ELEANORA IN PIECES

JESSICA MAFFETORE

Black Rose Writing | Texas

©2024 by Jessica Maffetore
All rights reserved. No part of this book may be reproduced, stored in a retrieval system or transmitted in any form or by any means without the prior written permission of the publishers, except by a reviewer who may quote brief passages in a review to be printed in a newspaper, magazine or journal.

The author grants the final approval for this literary material.

First printing

This is a work of fiction. Names, characters, businesses, places, events, and incidents are either the products of the author's imagination or used in a fictitious manner. Any resemblance to actual persons, living or dead, or actual events is purely coincidental.

ISBN: 978-1-68513-471-6
LIBRARY OF CONGRESS CONTROL NUMBER: 2024934274
PUBLISHED BY BLACK ROSE WRITING
www.blackrosewriting.com

Printed in the United States of America
Suggested Retail Price (SRP) $19.95

Eleanora in Pieces is printed in Book Antiqua

*As a planet-friendly publisher, Black Rose Writing does its best to eliminate unnecessary waste to reduce paper usage and energy costs, while never compromising the reading experience. As a result, the final word count vs. page count may not meet common expectations.

Cover Design by Sofia Iudina

PRAISE FOR ELEANORA IN PIECES

"Jessica Maffetore draws the reader in with lyrical descriptions of loss, grief, anger and frustration. Her masterful pacing of heavy moments to light kept me immersed…I read the book in two days."
–**Cheri Krueger, author of** *The Abduction of Adrienne Berg*

"Maffetore paints Ellie's world with the vivid prose of an artist. There is beauty in the horror that doesn't let us look away, even as we ache for Ellie to make better choices, to understand that life is full of second chances.

Full of emotional depth, *Eleanora in Pieces* will have you turning pages late into the night. Highly recommend."
–**Marisa Rae Dondlinger, author of** *Come and Get Me*

"In her debut novel, *Eleanora in Pieces*, Jessica Maffetore has created a poignant portrait of loss, redemption, and the relationships that tear us apart and bring us together. Maffetore's novel is an inspirational exploration of family, friendship, and the indomitable strength of the human spirit."
–**Troy Hollan, author of** *Clucked*

"This all too real tale of child abduction will have you turning pages, hoping and wondering how it will all turn out. Highly recommend for the well-written characters and the unexpected plot twists. 5 Stars."
–**Gail Olmsted, author of** *Miranda Writes, Miranda Nights*, **etc.**

"Bravo to Maffetore for writing a stunning and intricately shaped novel about how we handle loss and yet keep on living."
–**Dawn Reno Langley, author of** *Analyzing the Prescotts*

"…a raw, agonizing, but masterfully scripted tale. I have always prided myself on being empathetic towards women, but after reading this, I realize that I didn't have a clue. Perhaps as a man, I never can, but this is a book that although written primarily for women, should also be required reading for men. I highly recommend it!"
–**Bill Schweitzer, author of** *Doves in a Tempest*

"Beautifully written, heart wrenching, but ultimately hopeful, this novel takes readers through the indescribable grief of Eleanora whose son was taken from his bed and has been missing for years. Mafferore's ability to understand and describe the complex emotions of this grieving mother are incredibly moving and devastatingly accurate. A wonderful debut by a very talented writer."
–**Kim McCollum, author of** *What Happens in Montana*

"Maffetore's excellent storytelling puts us in her pain and makes us long for the answers and the purpose that the main character so desperately needs. Five Stars."
–**Yvonne DeSousa, author of** *Shelter of the Monument*

For my grandmother,
Mary Benton Gemmell
Thank you, a thousand times over,
for sharing your love of books with all of us.

ELEANORA
IN PIECES

PROLOGUE

The closest way I can describe it is the feeling of thinking there is one more step in the staircase…that stomach-dropping rush as your foot keeps moving through the empty air when your body expects it to stop. I knew where his body should be, so often had I felt it there before. But instead of warm skin and a sweaty swatch of hair sticking up above the blanket, I felt nothing, my outstretched hand falling in a sickening drop to land on the empty mattress.

I didn't turn on the hall light anymore when I checked on him. Now that he was older and so close to his 5th birthday, he was more sensitive to interruptions in the night and would ask me to leave it on if he happened to wake. He had caught enough glimpses of the evening news and ads for scary movies to know that frightening things existed in the world. Each day brought about a new 'Is it real?' question. Are ghosts real? Are vampires real? Are volcanoes real? Are heroes real? *Usually, the answers were simple enough and reassuring to him.*

This is not to say he didn't catch me off guard sometimes. 'Are bad guys real, Mommy?' he had asked. It broke my heart to say yes and watch his eyes fill with fear like rising water. We talked about not speaking to strangers and locking our doors and trusting the police to keep us safe. But somehow, these were harder ideas to grasp than bad guys on the loose.

So, we stuck with bedtime stories and extra goodnight kisses and checking for monsters under the bed, and soon, he would drop peacefully into sleep, tucked in a ball in the center of the mattress. Still, I was a young mother who had just survived his vulnerable infancy and needed to check on him before I could rest. One last confirmation that he was breathing, making sure his blanket was straight and his stuffed animals were securely tucked under his arm so he wouldn't wake in the night reaching out for them. This is what I told myself, though I knew he no longer needed me in that way. And so, each night I stole into his dark room on whisper-quiet feet to place a hand on his sleeping form one last time before I went to bed.

I used to have nightmares sometimes that he was gone. That I would fail at the most basic requirement of parenting. That I would turn around in a store and he would have vanished. That I would search every inch of the playground after losing sight of him for a second and never find him. That he would choke or slip and hit his small head or step into a busy street at the wrong moment.

I imagine every parent gives free reign to these thoughts every so often — allowing themselves to contemplate the worst, imagine the horror. The presence of him, the warmth of his breath, his sticky hand in mine, his piping voice all chased the nightmares away and fed the sense of security I tried to build around us.

Until he was gone. And then, everything was gone.

CHAPTER 1

She is the third therapist. No words can quite capture the strange, mismatched way she is dressed. Stranger than hipster, more disorganized than boho, louder than eccentric. There is a riot of color, layers of patterns. Clearly, no thought was given to the coordination of paisley top and floral bottom or neon sock and pastel shoe. I wonder if she thinks this makes her seem more intellectual. Like she is too busy thinking deep thoughts to worry about her clothing. It is an outward distraction in a place where I am supposed to be inwardly focused.

Her name is Jane, which I like, as far as names go. The first two therapists had names I didn't like, and that made it harder to concentrate. I realize the stupidity of this, but I didn't want to be there in the first place, so I cling to any excuse.

The first one—*Call me Dr. Carl,* he said—wanted me to stop carrying Owen's picture in my wallet. Dr. Carl's bleach-scented office was sandwiched between a physical therapist and an orthopedic surgeon in a medical building, meaning I almost always ended up holding the front door for someone limping in behind me on a pair of crutches or wearing some kind of torturous-looking knee brace. The light coming through the one small window beside his desk was mostly blocked by a large, artificial ficus tree–the only decoration in the whole room–and a rack of pamphlets with titles like *"Identifying Obsessive*

Compulsive Behavior," "Stress Management in a Busy World," "Removing the Disorder from Post Traumatic Stress," and "Social Anxiety and You."

Dr. Carl, a spindly man in his late 60s, thought I should focus on "life moving forward." He suggested I paint Owen's room or better yet, sell my house. Leave the place my son disappeared from. I shifted in the squeaky, vinyl-covered chair he provided for his patients and told him I didn't see these as viable options. He, from behind the solid wall of his thick-rimmed glasses and his buttoned-to-the-collar shirt, asked me to try. I left.

The second therapist's name was Miss Beverly. Like a schoolteacher or a debutante. I tried to keep my face still as she shook my hand with just the tips of her icy fingers when I arrived for our first session at her tiny, fully wall-papered home office. Stepping around a knee-high pile of knitting magazines and a fur covered pillow that looked like it normally held a smallish pet–I was guessing cat, she definitely seemed like a cat person–I took a seat on the pink velour sofa. A wave of throat-burning smoke rose from the lilac and lavender candles burning in a row along a low coffee table.

She smiled, patting her hair-sprayed dome of blonde hair into place, and asked me to tell her about my day, which is how she started each of the twelve sessions I completed with her before I quit the suffocating hell of that place. I didn't quit because of her name, or because of the candles or the hair. I quit because in twelve sessions, spread across twelve weeks, she wore the same cream-colored pantsuit that hugged her bulging middle and had a row of gold buttons down the front decorated with tiny gold anchors. I found it impossible to believe she didn't have any other clothes to wear. Not when she charged $175 an hour. The outfit drove me insane but I couldn't bring myself to ask about it. It was rude, and I don't like to be rude.

Miss Beverly had suggested I go to support group meetings, consider becoming a motivational speaker or an inspirational writer for other grieving parents, or perhaps help my sister, Geneva, with In Owen's Honor, the charity foundation she had started in my son's name. She wanted me to share my situation, help others learn from it, find peace through work. I did not agree.

So now I'm giving mismatched Jane a chance. Her office is actually quite nice. Peaceful and calming, it's decorated in shades of pale blues and greens and tans, with abstract watercolor paintings on the walls and wide windows covered with gauzy curtains. Likewise, Jane seems fine so far, relatively inoffensive from what I can tell. She's maybe in her mid-40s, medium height, light brown hair cut into a smooth bob, no noticeable birthmarks or strange disfigurements. It's just the lack of clothing coordination, which is still way better than wearing the same thing every day. *God, what is wrong with me?* I feel a wash of shame for my silent assessment of this person who is here to help me. I wish, not for the first time, that it was normal to drink a glass of wine at therapy. *Wouldn't everyone be so much more relaxed?*

I have to work to focus on the questions Jane is gently poking me with.

"What do you want out of therapy?" she asks.

What does anyone want? A normally functioning brain. A day without hating myself. A mask so I can pretend to be someone else. A way to erase 99% of my thoughts. Are any of those possible?

"Why are you here?" she insists.

Because I'm crazy? Because everyone says I should be here? Because some days I can't eat, some days I can't sleep? Because some days all I do is eat and sleep? Because some days there doesn't seem to be enough air around me to catch my breath? I don't know.

What I do know is that Owen is gone. I know that I put him to bed on a Monday night, like I always did, went to take a shower, and when I checked on him an hour later, he was gone. I know that February 9th was the last day I saw him, 41 days before his fifth birthday. I know these things in the same way I know my hair is brown. They are facts. Things I have seen written down and heard told to me. What I don't know, what no one can tell me, is what happened to my baby. People say I lost him. *Sorry for the loss of your son.* Or, *so unfair to lose a child so young, only four years old.* They mean condolence. I hear accusation.

Did I lose Owen? Misplace him? That is saying that he is located somewhere else, somewhere findable. Here's where I can't tell reality from make-believe, and one of the biggest reasons every day seems so intolerably long, so undeniably tortuous. The facts — the ones the reporters voiced over and over and the cameras showed in a voyeuristic loop in the weeks following his disappearance — say that he is most likely dead, *presumed* dead. I read somewhere that if an abducted child is not found within the first three hours of being taken, then the likelihood of them being found alive drops to almost nothing.

But the truth is that no one knows just where he is.

I have not laid my child's body in the ground or seen his face devoid of life and gently closed his eyes forever, as is my right as his mother. So yes, he is still out there waiting. Waiting for me to find him. But hardly anyone believes this. The worst is when people tell me he is in a better place. This makes me want to calmly place my purse on the nearest flat surface and punch them in the mouth. I have refrained so far, but I make no promises in that regard.

Jane asks me if there is anything in particular I want to talk about. I narrow my eyes at her, thinking she is being smart. Everyone knows about Owen. I have been on TV a hundred times–on the local stations where we live here in Newton, Massachusetts, to the larger Boston stations, to the national network news across the country, and online around the world.

My face and his face, everywhere for people to see, my name and his name in conversations I hear at the grocery store in our neighborhood or falling from the lips of strangers on the street.

The words follow me in invisible waves of whispers as I walk anywhere in public: *missing... little boy... where was his mother?... poor kid...* There is always the subtle insinuation that I had something to do with it, though the police have publicly stated that I was not involved in his disappearance. The idea crushes me until I actually feel my heart ground down into an unrecognizable smudge in my chest.

I eye Jane. Of course she knows. I had written *dealing with the disappearance of my 4-year-old son* on the registration paperwork when I made the appointment. She is asking if I want to start there. If Owen is my whole existence, my whole struggle, my whole mental issue. *Sure it is*, I think. Some hollow place inside of me laughs.

The moments after I realize he is gone are blurry, with a loud buzzing sound in my ears like the roar of a thousand jet engines. Every room in the house is empty. He's not in the bathroom, he's not hiding under the kitchen table. He's not here.

Time goes in slow-motion as I run from room to room. My hair, still wet from the shower, clings to my face and my neck, leaving a dark ring around the neck of the t-shirt I had planned to wear to bed. I can feel the rush of cold air through the back door and the punch of fear in my stomach when the truth of that open door hits me. Open and unlocked. I can feel the strain in my throat as I scream his name, but I can't hear the sound of my own voice.

The grass is wet under my bare feet. Cold February air crystallizes every ragged breath but I don't feel it on my skin. The night is dark, the dim moonlight barely casting enough light to see the outline of the neighbors' houses. I spin frantically in a circle, not knowing which way to go, where to look. Did he wander away? Did he go looking for a lost toy or the stray cat we see in our yard sometimes? It's so cold. He wouldn't come out here. He never has before.

Dear God.

I cry his name over and over, slipping on the grass, desperate to go in every direction at once.

CHAPTER 2

I hand Daniel his coffee every morning when he walks in the kitchen.

"Thank you," he always says, and I nod in return.

It feels like a very ordinary, very uninteresting business transaction. The fact that it takes place in the sunny kitchen of the house my husband and I share doesn't make it any warmer. I stopped drinking coffee two years ago. It burns my stomach, which has plagued me since Owen's been gone. At times, my stomach rejects food all together, violently shoving it back up where it came from as if it is horrified that I dare to eat. Other times, it feels bottomless and empty, so bowls of food and bottles of wine disappear into it in alarming quantities. I've lost and regained the same fifteen pounds half a dozen times.

But I still make Daniel his coffee, even though the smell torments me. I linger in the kitchen while he drinks it, watching him as he sits at the kitchen table, scrolling the news on his phone or tapping out emails on his laptop before getting in his car to drive the ten miles to where he works in one of those new office buildings in Boston's Seaport District.

At some point, Daniel stopped kissing me goodbye in the mornings. Instead, he leaves with a wave or quick goodbye, the words half lost as the door closes behind him. He skirts around me much of the time, having learned that attempting physical contact opens a door on the stuff he would rather avoid. I want his closeness; his actual presence is more comforting than anything. But that is all. I just want to take the comfort, feel his shoulder under my head, absorb his smell and his strength and his being. I have nothing to give back to him, and it is clear from his growing indifference to me that he is growing tired of it. I am watching our marriage wilt like a dying garden that I have no strength to water.

Any attempt Daniel has made to initiate intimacy in the past two years has failed miserably. As much as I want to be there for him, give him what he needs, I end up a sobbing, emotional mess. Anything inside of me that used to feel joy, or longing, or God forbid, passion, is wrapped up tight in a straitjacket of tension and guilt; constricted, tense and bound with no possibility of relaxation or release. Pleasure is the absolute last thing I can imagine feeling.

Dr. Carl, who was very keen on knowing about my sex life–the voyeuristic prick–said these feelings would return in time if I let them. I'm not sure Daniel will wait that long. Miss Beverly suggested more hand holding and "non-intercourse affection." Sure, brilliant.

Daniel is not Owen's father. I could say he's the closest thing Owen ever had, but that implies that Daniel acted like a father when that's not exactly true. He was a father-by-proximity in that they both existed in the same space at certain times. But they hadn't bonded in the ways I had hoped for when I first brought Daniel home to meet my son.

I had so much faith. When I think about myself at that time, it reminds me of one of those laundry detergent commercials. Some idiotic blonde woman prancing through a field of flowers in a flowy skirt, since she apparently has nothing better to do than celebrate her clean clothes. I was floaty and empty and brainless back then. I thought I could manufacture a family. Instead, I created a tolerable roommate situation.

My relationship with Daniel was almost totally separate from my relationship with my son, like a Venn diagram with *very minutely* overlapping circles. Daniel was a friend of a friend. Someone thought we would be good together. He didn't balk at the fact that I was a single mother, didn't care that I came with baggage. He was divorced but not bitter, smart but not too serious, at least back then. We found a lot to talk about. We left Owen with my parents for long weekends and went to the Cape or Newburyport. We ate brunch. Spent mornings in bed. Shopped for things we didn't need. And then he went home to his apartment in Cambridge and got to be a grown up, while I went back to the reality of life with a little boy in the house I had bought for us after I found out I was pregnant.

Knowing the third floor, one-bedroom apartment I had been renting in Brookline would not work with a baby, I had moved back to my hometown of Newton before Owen was born. As much as I didn't want to admit it, being close to my parents, who still lived in the house where I grew up, and my sister, who lived across town in one of the nicest neighborhoods in the city, was going to be very handy. While Brookline was a convenient train ride from Boston, and from my office, Newton was still close enough to make everything work. And I was earning enough money to afford a recently renovated, two-story, three-bedroom colonial on a quiet street, with a row of flowering cherry trees in the front, and a wide lawn in the back.

It wasn't long before I was bringing Daniel there to spend time together, drawing him into the safe space I had built for Owen and I, filled with his leaky juice cups, messy art projects on the fridge and bright plastic toddler toys scattered from one end of the house to the other. It was a far cry from our leisurely grown-up dates but I knew I could make it work. I loved both of them. And Daniel, while not necessarily the instantly perfect step-father, seemed ok with the idea.

After a year of dating, we got married at city hall. My mother, born and raised on the south coast of Italy until she married my father and they moved to America in 1974, sobbed and swore I would go to hell if I didn't get married in the Catholic church. She cried again when I didn't wear white. She must have forgotten she had already told me I was damned for having Owen out of wedlock. My poor mother. She has cried so much for me, positive that God won't love me any more for all the wrongs I've done. But she came to the wedding anyway and insisted on hosting a small dinner at her house to "celebrate." She wiped tears from her cheeks as she cooked the food in her kitchen, but pulled it together long enough for my father to stiffly toast the new couple. Owen wore a little blue vest and tie. He was too young to actually hold the rings, but I told myself he was the ring bearer. And that I was making a good choice for his future. And mine. Daniel moved into our house, and I tried to make it a home for the three of us.

I don't know much about Owen's real dad. I met him while I was traveling for work. I never asked his last name. He said he was from California, but not what part. Other than the fact that he was blonde and tall, I couldn't tell you many more details about him. We sat next to each other in a conference session called *Maximizing the Output of Your Sales Team in 3 Easy Steps!* I took notes, and he watched me, tapping long fingers on his knee when the session ran over time. When it ended, he asked what session I was headed to next and then walked with me there, making polite conference-appropriate conversation. *Where was I from? How long had I been in sales? What did I think of the conference so far?*

When the next session let out, he was standing outside, searching the crowd with his gorgeous blue eyes, which lit up when he saw me. He asked to buy me a drink. He was wearing a green button-up shirt and looked me right in the eye over his Miller Light. Several drinks later, I excused myself to run to the ladies' room where I checked my breath and silently thanked God that I was wearing decent underwear and had remembered to shave my legs that morning.

I let him kiss me in the elevator on the way up to my room. The rest is pretty damn predictable, right down to the part where I was too shy to ask if he had a condom. I was stupid and drunk and got pregnant. I have zero excuse for being so irresponsible. None. Everyone thought he would reappear when Owen went missing, except for me. I never told him I was pregnant. I was embarrassed and didn't know how to find him and didn't know what the actual fuck I was doing. He had gone his way, and I had gone mine, never imagining that the details of a one-night stand would become so important.

The police pushed very hard to find him after Owen disappeared, even going back and finding the registration list for the conference we had attended. But all I had was a first name, Craig. And he had either lied about his name, which hadn't occurred to me until that point, or he wasn't registered, because no Craigs appeared on the registration list. That part didn't bother me. He didn't take Owen. I knew he didn't.

My parents' devastation when I told them I was pregnant knew no end. That is, until I laid that child in their arms. There is a point where even parental disappointment sprinkled with a good helping of moral judgment can be mollified by the tiny fingers, fat pink cheeks, and sweet little cries of a new grandchild. They had softened toward me after he was born. But I was, have no doubt, the ultimate failure as a child. Despite their outcry over the city hall wedding, I know they were relieved when I married Daniel. It meant they could pass us off as a real family, free from shame. We could be seen in public, Daniel on one side of me, Owen on the other. Each taking one of my hands and holding on to half of me at the same time.

CHAPTER 3

The two-year anniversary of Owen's disappearance is approaching. I plow toward it, headlong, knowing I will have to face its significance. The time he has been gone exists in a different reality. Some hours stretch so intolerably long I think I'll suffocate before they end. I also live through many days of which I have no memory. I look at a calendar and can't reconcile the actual date with how much time has passed. My therapy appointments are like anchors, even though I despise them. I like having something on the calendar. I write the appointment time in giant letters so that it takes up the whole box, as if I have *big* plans that will last all day. The other boxes are empty.

I don't have to mark his anniversary on the calendar. I know, down to the minute, when I lost him. I know what I fed him for dinner that night. I know how long his hair was, curling like the softest bird feathers against his neck, and what show I had let him watch before bed while I washed the dishes. I know the color of the pajamas he was wearing. They didn't match, of course. They never did. He didn't like to wear the matching set. Little blue sharks on the top, green and orange stripes on the bottom. Or the Spiderman t-shirt with Pokémon shorts. It drove me nuts, but he loved it. It was one of the small things he could control, and the look of pride on his face when he ran out of his room proudly donning his newest combination was too adorable to try to correct. So, I have a white shirt with dogs in Santa hats, and a pair of bottoms with yellow Batman logos. And Owen is wearing the mismatching pair.

Of course, they would be too small for him by now. Geneva makes that point when she comes over on the weekend to go over the charity event schedule for the upcoming year. Not that I plan on attending any of them.

"You still have all his clothes and things?" she asks in her obnoxiously gentle big sister voice, peering into his room. We had come upstairs so she could look at the fixtures in my bathrooms. She and her husband were remodeling their guest bath and were looking for inspiration. Uninvited, she had stopped at Owen's room and swung the door open.

Cursing myself for leaving the door unlatched, I look away, hating the practiced pity in her eyes. She takes my hands in hers and calmly explains how much I would help another family in need by donating all of Owen's things.

"Imagine how much joy they would bring!" she insists, tears brimming in her eyes. "Wouldn't Owen have wanted that?" I let my own eyes glaze over, looking through her, refusing to participate in the conversation.

"C'mon Ellie, he'll have outgrown all these things even if...." but she doesn't say the rest. She doesn't believe that he will come home. No one does, except for me. I turn and silently retreat down the stairs.

"Am I supposed to get rid of his clothes?" I ask Jane in our third therapy session. Her eyes widen slightly, but she keeps the rest of her face still.

I'm guessing she would describe me as difficult up to this point, given the chance. We haven't discussed much more than family history so far. My parents, my upbringing, my sister. With fifteen minutes to go in our last appointment, she asked if

I wanted to talk about my son. *Of course, I do*, I wanted to scream. *What else is worth talking about??* I had avoided her gaze, looking out the window instead. Because the answer is also no. No, I don't want to talk about him. What else is there to say? I failed, I lost him, he's gone. End of story. Every time I talk about him, it comes back to the same thing. The same sorrow, the same empty. The same pieces of me, torn apart and hopelessly scattered. I let the silence string out so long that Jane eventually turned to another topic and let it go.

My question today is clearly the opening she has been waiting for, so she is careful in her response. She thinks about it for a long minute, examining me from behind the huge cowl neck of her bright yellow sweater. She wears this over a red plaid skirt that ends well above her chunky embroidered boots. I have to work hard not to look at her clothes, lest she think I am judging her. It takes considerable effort. She certainly is a colorful woman. Finally, she speaks.

"I don't think there is any *supposed to* in these situations," she says. I can feel the doubt showing on my face. She clears her throat.

"Eleanora, I could give you a whole load of bullshit about how things are just things and they don't represent your son, but I know it doesn't feel that way. You have to be ready," she says. I smile a little. I like that she said bullshit. It clashes so badly with her outfit.

I leave Jane's office and go to Target for laundry detergent and tissues and shampoo. But first I have to walk through the toy aisles. And the boys' clothing section. Normally, I just pass through. Maybe a brief pause to examine a Star Wars figure or a stuffed Spiderman. The toys are so new and clean. I imagine filling my cart, wrapping packages for Christmas or his birthday, hearing his squeals of happiness when he rips the paper open. He'll throw himself into my arms for a big hug if I pick out exactly the right thing for him. I leave quickly when other children appear.

I wander through the racks of boys' clothes. Owen's not four-almost-five anymore. He's six-almost-seven. I hold up a pair of size 7/8 green sweatpants with white piping down the leg. When I last had him, Owen was still in 5T sizes. T for toddler. Still a baby. Such a little peanut. I try to imagine him bigger, wider than he was. He was growing so fast back in those days. I can't reconcile the size of the pants with my child. I know that, if I find him, his clothes won't fit any more. *When I find him.* I turn the pants this way and that. Measuring, stretching, estimating. I fold the pants neatly and put them in my cart.

I feel a small warmth inside, like I've done the right thing. Part of me wants so desperately to be ready when Owen comes home. How horrible would it be if he comes back and has outgrown everything—his clothes, his shoes, the easy-reader books he was beginning to sound out. Maybe he will have learned to read really well by now. Maybe even chapter books. He definitely won't want to play with his blocks and big chunky plastic trucks. He'll have moved on.

When a teenager in a red vest and name tag asks if I need help, I realize I'm standing still in the middle of the aisle on the other side of the store, with tears free-flowing down my face. I look down. My cart is full, almost overflowing. Toys and games. Lunch box snacks and Golden Grahams. Frozen chicken nuggets shaped like dinosaurs, string cheese, and strawberry-flavored Danimals yogurt. Packages of little boy underwear with SpongeBob and The Hulk on them. Blue Velcro sneakers and a stack of different colored boys' sweatshirts. A whole new wardrobe, in fact.

My cheeks flame red. I can't remember doing this, filling the cart with everything I would need for Owen if he came home. The handle of the cart leaves a deep sweaty groove across my palms when I unclench my fingers to look at my watch. It's almost five o'clock. Hours have gone by. I can't remember them passing. The girl in the vest is staring at me. I hastily wipe my face, smile weakly at her, and insist I'm fine. I leave my cart in the aisle and walk out of the store, using every bit of will power I have to stop myself from breaking into a desperate, sobbing run.

CHAPTER 4

On an average day, after Daniel leaves for work, I shower and put on a pair of yoga pants–greatest invention ever, if you ask me, not that I've ever done any amount of yoga in them. I then get through a few hours of work, sitting at our kitchen table. Usually, I don't have to interact with anyone, something I am very grateful for. I'm sure my boss talks about me behind my back. I mean, who wouldn't? She's nice enough, but even I have to admit that I've more than taken advantage of the situation. I'm late handing in reports. I don't answer emails right away. And I have the most amazing list of excuses for not coming into the office for team meetings. She never gives me a hard time, but I don't know how much longer she will put up with it.

I used to work in sales, selling medical equipment to hospitals and physicians' offices. I liked to tell myself back then that I was helping people, but that was a stretch. However, I was one of the top performers on the sales team. And I liked my job. I used to enjoy talking to people. I was friendly, even. I had no problem pounding the phones, visiting doctors in between their appointments, or sweet-talking hospital admins who prided themselves on being stingy with their budgets. Now, I can't stand the idea. I have lost the ability to fake-smile.

I took six months off work. I had so much to do, but I don't remember a lot of it. So many police interviews and meetings and search parties and questions. So, so many questions to answer. I don't remember telling Flavia, my boss, what had happened. Maybe Daniel had made that call. Or maybe she had seen the news reports. But I didn't hear from her until six or maybe eight weeks later.

"*Hey Ellie, I know it's rough going right now, but maybe work would be a good distraction?*" she had said. "*I'm not rushing you, just want to put it out there. You are always welcome to come back when you are ready.*"

I wasn't ready then. I'm still not ready now. Not ready to confidently pitch a new product, haggle over pricing, or extol the amazing capabilities of this new machine or that one. It involves too much eye contact, too much effort, too much hollowness. I know I'm not helping anyone. I'm not making the world a better place. So, the effort is just too much.

I didn't explain this to Flavia. I just told her I didn't have the energy for sales anymore. She said she understood and offered to let me work from home as an operations analyst, doing reporting and account maintenance for the other sales reps. It was an unusual career move, and I certainly didn't have the training for it. But I knew Flavia had made the offer out of pity and I took it, understanding from Daniel's ever-less-gentle reminders that we had bills to pay.

I also need something to do with my brain. The reporting is nice, in a way. Numbers make sense. Reps either make or don't make their quotas. Pluses or minuses. There is very little gray area. When I worked sales, there was always so much up in the air. *Did you close that deal yet? Is that prospect going to sign? How much pipeline can we generate this quarter? What's the best discount you can offer?* So much room for *maybe*s and *we'll see*s. Any day could end up being a win, eligible for celebration, or just another day of waiting and hoping and breath-holding. Now, there is none of that. Only reliable, solid, quiet numbers that don't even belong to me, so I don't give a shit about them. They are completely void of emotion. And for a few hours a day, everything adds up at the bottom of the spreadsheet. If they don't, I can find the mistake, retrace my steps, identify what went wrong, and fix it. Imagine that.

A few days before Owen's anniversary I get a meeting invite from Flavia. The subject line is all caps, with lots of asterisks, calling for a mandatory, all-company meeting on Thursday. *Ugh. Real pants*, is my first thought. I mentally scroll through possible excuses. Therapy? Flavia can't possibly be mad if I am busy working on my mental health. No, Flavia knows therapy is on Tuesdays. I've got my appointments blocked in my calendar so I can't be booked for work meetings. I could be sick. Or out of town, not that I ever go anywhere. I've gotten away with only going into the office three or four times in the past year, and I'm not excited to up that score. I look at the invite again. *All-hands company meeting – we need the whole team present. Please rearrange your schedules to accommodate. No exceptions.* Fuck.

"I don't want to go," I say to Daniel when he gets home from work that night. I'm standing at the kitchen counter, cutting up carrots for a salad, my back to him. "I shouldn't have to." He, of course, goes to meetings every single day. Has grown-up conversations. Looks people in the eye. But he doesn't have the same stain on him that I do, doesn't get the same stares, or the same judgment.

"Why not?" he asks as he grabs a jar of roasted nuts from the cabinet and starts picking through them. I look over my shoulder at him with raised eyebrows until he glances up at the silence and understanding slowly hits him. Thursday is Owen's anniversary. He hasn't forgotten, it has just taken him a minute to put two and two together. He comes across the small kitchen and puts an arm around my shoulders.

"Sorry, kiddo, but you can't expect them to remember that, right?" he says.

I chop faster, sending uneven chunks of carrot flying across the counter. I don't expect anyone, other than Daniel and my family, to remember. Except they will. It will happen just like it did last year. News vans in front of our house, phone calls for interviews, everyone reminding everyone else that it has been a full year, now two years, since that little boy went missing. *Can you believe there have been no leads?* And *no sign of him, really?* And let's try to get a look at his mother's face to see if we can detect any sign of guilt, any trace of happiness that she might dare to feel even though they haven't found her son. Let's make sure she is still thinking about him even if, every other day of the year, the rest of us have forgotten.

Daniel watches my face as all these thoughts slam around inside my head. He sighs and puts the nuts back in the cabinet. He comes back and puts a hand on either shoulder, using his thumbs to rub small circles at the base of my neck. I continue to savagely attack the carrots.

"It will probably be good for you to get out of the house," he says. "And maybe, I dunno, not answer the phone?"

I stop chopping, the knife still in my hand. I know Daniel is tired; I can hear it in his voice. Tired of me the way that I am. Tired of tears. Tired of excuses. Tired of the sadness that has taken over our home for the last two years. I feel for him, with what little empathy I can squeeze out. I close my eyes and remind myself that he wants to help. Deep breath. He stops rubbing.

"You are probably right," I say, not sounding as sincere as I was hoping.

Later that night, while Daniel is washing dishes and whistling a Phish song under his breath, I click "Accept" on the meeting invite and go search for a pair of pants that fit.

CHAPTER 5

Owen spent the first few weeks of his life sleeping in my arms. He was tiny and hungry and completely unwilling to sleep in the bassinet or car seat or crib. When placed down, he would wake within minutes and scream his face red. The instant I picked him up, he would stop and slip back into sleep in his endearing, infuriating, exhausting way.

I was so sleep deprived I began falling asleep the moment I sat down anywhere. One evening, I lay down on the couch, Owen sleeping soundly on my chest. Seconds later, I was out so deeply I didn't realize I had shifted, didn't feel his body slip down between me and the couch. Didn't feel his struggles or hear his muffled crying. I don't know how long he was there. But by the time his movements eventually woke me and the panic of not finding him where I'd left him flashed through my body and I pulled him up, his face was turning blue. He took a gulp of air and let out the loudest and most beautiful scream I had ever heard.

I couldn't stop crying. I tried to control the sobs so I wouldn't disturb Owen, who was now curled around my breast, soothing himself with a meal, but my throat burned with horror and fear. The realization that it only took a moment of carelessness to put him in danger left my whole body weak and trembling.

I didn't tell anyone about this failure, this close call—the shame was too great. How could someone ever think of me as a good mother, knowing I had done such a thing to my own son? So I tucked it into a ball and buried it deep inside of me, pretending it hadn't happened. Every so often the memory would billow up like steam, fast and unexpected, and burn through my mind: his clammy cheek, his limp body, and the rush of adrenaline-laden relief at realizing he was ok. Then the flood of guilt that I had failed him.

Guilt wasn't a new feeling for me. I was an expert at it, thanks in part to my mother, who never failed to remind me of my shortcomings. I could never allow myself to enjoy being the recipient of a favor. Instead, I evaluated and tallied and mentally noted exactly how to pay the giver back so there was no chance of them thinking I had failed to make things even. But the guilt of motherhood brought with it new depths of these feelings. A whole, yet-unknown list of things I could fail at.

I used to care a lot about failing at work. The idea of not reaching my quota was so terrifying that I worked my ass off to make sure I hit my numbers way ahead of schedule. Then I still sweated out the last few weeks of the quarter, trying to make sure I sold more than everyone else. I didn't want anyone to think I couldn't keep up with the rest of the team, most of whom were men. They were uncomfortable with me around; they didn't know how to treat me. I wasn't one of the guys, grabbing beers after work, celebrating wins with tequila shots at their desks, or digging into deep conversations about the performance of the Patriots' offensive line this season. Instead, I showed up, gave them a lot of hell, and took off at the end of the day, especially after Owen was born. As long as I consistently topped the leader board, I didn't care about anything else. I could joke around enough that the guys generally liked me but more or less left me alone. It worked for me.

Now, more than ever, they have absolutely no idea how to act around me. There's no joking around, no bragging or swaggering, and definitely no invites for beers after work. Maybe if I was there every day, people would have grown used to me, used to the changes in me. Instead, they ignore me for the most part. Most don't even say hello. The few that do nod a quick greeting or chirp out a "Hey Ellie," before quickly moving past, not wanting to risk a longer interaction. Even Katie and Ellen from the marketing department, who I used to hit the Whole Foods salad bar with at lunchtime, take the long way around when they see me coming. It's exhausting, and a good excuse to continue avoiding the office.

Thursday comes, and I'm dreading the meeting even more. I've procrastinated getting ready so long that I'm rushing by the end to leave on time. I don't have time to do more than run a comb through my damp hair. After almost two years of completely neglecting it, I had recently grown frustrated with the constant mess of untamed waves and chopped most of the length off to just above my shoulders. Relieved of the annoyance, I went immediately back to neglecting it, meaning most days it sits in a half-hearted bun on top of my head, or hangs down in messy tangles. Today, I push it ineffectively behind each ear, resigned to it being good enough for one work meeting.

My work clothes are uncomfortable and tight, and I feel awkward in them, like I've squeezed into someone else's skin. I've become so unused to wearing heels that, when I slip them on, I don't last longer than the walk across the bedroom. I return immediately to the closet, kick them off into the pile of other rejected clothes that has formed this morning in the middle of the floor, and opt for a pair of flats, office etiquette be damned.

Downstairs, as I grab my purse and keys and turn to swing the front door shut behind me, the house phone rings. I freeze, as I always do. From where I'm standing at the front door I can see through the living room into the kitchen where the phone sits on the counter just next to the fridge, lighting up with every ring. I hold my breath, waiting to see if it will stop. I always answer the phone. Always. Even when Daniel gives me that *How desperate can a person be?* look.

We wouldn't have a house phone at all if it were up to Daniel, but I insist. We need a publicly published phone number in case someone needs to get in touch with us about Owen. It was hard when he first went missing and every reporter in the world was calling and every other person wanted to tell us they had seen a boy who looked like Owen at a playground in Austin or at an airport in Bogotá.

I used to work with the reporters, describing him over and over, even though they had his picture. Pleading with them to keep asking the public for help. Begging them to show his face again and again, holding on to the hope that someone, somewhere knew where he was. I also heard out everyone that called with a tip, even though the police said not to talk to anyone. They claimed they would handle tips on their side since all the news channels were giving out their number for people to call anyway. But people found our home number and called us directly. I couldn't stand the idea of possibly missing the one call that would bring Owen home. So, the phone rings, and I answer it.

As time has gone by, the tide of phone calls has slowed further and further. Now they are hardly more than sporadic but are as unhelpful as they have always been. On Owen's one-year anniversary, the flood restarted, first the reporters and then, after people had been reminded of his sweet face in the news reports, the tips. Someone had seen him on a bus in Hartford. Another person insisted he was living in Florida with their next-door neighbor, who had been passing him off as their orphaned nephew. I took careful notes and handed them off to the police, as instructed. Every one of them led to a dead end.

Despite the record of complete failure and let-down, the sound of the phone still hits me in the gut every time with that wave of sickness that is part dread, part hope. I feel the rings cut through me as I stand there with the doorknob in one hand. One more ring, and I can't take it anymore. I sprint to the kitchen and grab the phone.

"Hello?" I ask, a bit breathless.

"Congratulations! You have been selected for a free stay at a Hilton Hotel. Press 1 to make your reserva—"

I hit the OFF button on the phone, missing, not for the first time, the good old days when you could slam a phone down to hang up on someone. I feel the usual wave of disappointment roll over me, and I squeeze my eyes shut to keep tears from forming. Daniel had warned me not to answer the phone this week, knowing that my nerves were even more on edge than normal. *Next one will be a reporter.* I walk stiffly back to the door and shut it behind me, not allowing myself to stop and reconsider. I know I'm seconds away from giving in to sweatpants and a mindless day of HGTV. *Not an option*, I tell myself and climb into my car.

By the time I get to the office, I'm about ten minutes late. None of the conference rooms are big enough for the whole company to fit in, so they've gathered everyone in the lobby, pulling up just enough chairs for the few older ladies who work in billing and the COO who looks to be seven or eight months pregnant. Everyone else is standing with their back to the glass front doors when I slip in, trying to go unnoticed. A few people turn to see who the latecomer is, but turn back when they see me. I spot Flavia up toward the front of the room, but she is listening intently to the CEO, who is standing on a chair by the reception desk in order to be heard.

Someone moves along the edge of the crowd toward me. Anton, a sales rep I've actually become friendly with, grins as he slides up next to me. He is one of the few coworkers I don't mind–one who doesn't treat me like a disease these days. In the past, we got along well and, after getting the work pleasantries out of the way, had real conversations that didn't involve sales, sports, or the weather. We drifted toward each other at company functions, quietly discussing the rest of our colleagues in covert tones as we sipped gin and tonics, Anton peering through his wire-rimmed glasses with feigned disgust as his over-optimistic counterparts flirted obnoxiously with the waitresses.

I know it is in part because he is jealous. At just over 5'6", Anton usually has to look up at me in my heels. Today, with me in flats, we are eye-to-eye. That, along with his thinning hair and fondness for anything at Starbucks that comes with whipped cream, means Anton tends to struggle a bit with dating. But, even so, he has a kind face with big dark eyes and an easy smile. He also makes me laugh. Or, at least, he used to, when laughing at work was a thing I did. I do, however, catch myself smiling a bit as he rolls his eyes in complaint of the long-winded CEO.

"What did I miss?" I whisper. Anton draws his finger across his neck.

"We're all dead," he whispers back. I frown. Last thing I need is drama.

"Now, I want to say here and now that there is nothing for ANY of you to be worried about," says the CEO, Barry Bonnar.

Barry owns a house on the Cape, another in Key West, and has never, in his life, found it necessary to set foot in a Walmart. He wears shirts that cost more than my monthly car payments. Both of his kids got automatic acceptance into Tufts, since the Bonnar family are not only alumni going back multiple generations, they have also donated enough funds over the years to have their name etched on several buildings. Besides our company, Barry also sits on the boards of three other companies and invests in various others. Barry has nothing to worry about.

"What's he talking about?" I whisper to Anton.

The big news is that the company has been acquired. Barry is pitching the story like it's the greatest thing to ever happen, ensuring everyone that this means more resources, more marketing dollars, and a larger network of providers to sell to. I glance around to see that not a single person in the crowd is buying it. We know what acquisition means. Barry concludes his cheerleader speech by saying it's business as usual with no immediate changes, but not to be worried if we start to see some new faces.

"The folks at Alcore are excited to get to know us, get to know our ways, and learn all about our success strategies!" he says, happily looking down at the sea of dismayed faces.

"Twenty bucks says that he is getting a fat buy-out of his contract," Anton says as the crowd begins to break up. "Companies don't need multiple CEOs."

I'm finding it hard to care and am slightly annoyed that Flavia made me come in for this. I think an email would have covered it, with a quick line at the bottom assuring me I still had a job. I'm glad, not for the first time, that my office visits are infrequent. I know this announcement will cause a lot of tension and many people will start job hunting, eager to not be the last one left on a sinking ship, even if it isn't actually a lost cause.

"You never know," I say. "It might be fine." Anton shrugs. We walk toward the cafeteria, where the head of HR has announced that they have generously ordered pizza for the whole company.

"Either way, things are going to change," he says.

He's right, and it makes me feel a slight wave of nausea. I can't stand change. Not anymore. I live for routine and comfort. My pants are pinching me, and I try not to be obvious about pulling at the waistband. I'll skip the pizza. Anton catches my pained look.

"How's things?" he asks, not trying to sound casual, but actually like he cares. "It's good to see you," he adds.

Strangely, I don't mind when Anton asks. He's not patronizing in the way that others are. I can tell that he doesn't think *I'm* a lost cause.

I shrug, though, not about to go into details in our current setting. I only get about three steps into the cafeteria before I can't make myself go any further. Hungry coworkers politely shoulder past and my head spins. I feel a flush rush up my neck and I fight the urge to run. I feel like everyone is staring, though they've continued to walk around me. Anton turns back when he realizes I'm no longer beside him. Catching the look on my face, he swings back in my direction, hooks his arm in mine, and pulls me out into the emptying hallway.

"C'mon," he says. "I have a better idea."

CHAPTER 6

There are no news vans parked outside the house. It might be the two, ok three, gin and tonics Anton and I had over lunch–I seriously should *not* have driven myself home–but it takes me several tries to check conclusively that there are no voicemails on the home phone either. I stand, swaying slightly, in the kitchen, trying to figure out if maybe Daniel has been home and erased them before I had the chance to get there. That would be like him, but it doesn't make sense. He'll still be at the office at this time. Plus, everyone should be gearing up for the five o'clock news and it's almost three now. They need time to pull their reports together, dig up Owen's photo, maybe have one of those artists draw an update of what he might look like now that he's two years older. But there's nothing. I know I haven't gotten the date wrong. I would know the day once it came, even without a calendar.

I'm still standing there, confused and frowning, when my cell phone rings. I dig through my purse, slightly reluctantly, to find it. My cell number is private, so I only get calls from people I know. I don't really want to talk to anyone at the moment. It's Geneva.

"Hi honey," she says sweetly. "Just checking in. You doing ok?" She sounds out of breath.

"No," I say.

"Oh, Ellie," Geneva sighs, and then grunts as if she's lifting something heavy.

"What are you doing?" I'm already annoyed with her.

"Just picking up the flower arrangements." I frown, as I flip through the mail. Last year, I received several condolence and thinking-of-you cards. This year there is only one–a small, pink envelope behind the stack of bills. I turn it over to see the return address.

"Uh huh," I say into the phone, not paying attention. The card is from my college friend, Anne. The sight of her name makes me smile. She is always so thoughtful.

"You'll love them," Geneva says cheerfully. "I think they will be a nice touch, all white with blue vases."

Anne's note is sweet and short, reminding me she's always there if I need her.

"White with blue…wait, what? What are you talking about?" I ask Geneva, checking back into the conversation. I can hear her car door slam through the phone.

"The flowers," she says slowly, as if I'm hard of hearing. "For the BE-NE-FIT. Tonight." I groan. I've totally forgotten. I open my mouth to protest.

"Don't even think about it, Ellie," Geneva says, knowing what I'm about to say. "You have to be there. It will be a good thing and everyone is expecting you."

"Genny, I can't…" I start to say, but she cuts me off.

"You're coming." Her tone sharpening. "Think of Owen."

I have to put the phone down on the kitchen table so that I don't throw it.

Geneva pisses me off, to say the least. She is everything that I'm not and always has been. Excelling at everything she tries, wildly successful in her career as a marketing executive at one of the biggest software companies in Boston, happily married to her handsome husband, Nathan, and raising her two tall, beautiful daughters in a huge house that is decorated like one of those homes on HGTV that looks perfect, but like no one actually lives there. Aside from being better than me at absolutely everything, she adores treating me like a child and has taken Owen's disappearance as an opportunity to play the hero.

Geneva started In Owen's Honor nine months after he had been gone. I was furious. You don't organize a foundation in someone's name if they are still alive. It felt like being forced to publicly accept that he was dead. She disagreed and pushed forward, without my blessing, insisting that she knew best. And now she holds immensely successful benefits to raise money for various children's causes, all in Owen's name, none of which have the slightest chance of helping to bring him home. Childhood cancer, St. Jude's, pediatric diabetes, Save the Children, No Kid Hungry, and so on. Geneva was a savior to them all. Except Owen. Even she can't help Owen.

I try to avoid attending the events that she organizes as often as I can, but sometimes she insists on my presence and I don't always have the heart to fight her. Some small part of me knows why she does it, knows that the events help her deal with the loss of her nephew. But they don't help me. They put me in the spotlight and remind a whole room full of people that I have failed to keep my son safe. Weepy mothers thank me for helping raise money for whatever illness has harmed or taken their own child. Awkward, uncomfortable fathers commend my bravery. Neighbors and family friends hand out hugs and shoulder squeezes. Teachers and first responders applaud our efforts, assuming I have something to do with planning. Those rooms never have enough air, or private corners to hide in. They have too many prying eyes and nauseatingly sympathetic head-tilts. As if I don't know what they all are thinking.

My parents do not attend these events. In fact, they want nothing to do with In Owen's Honor. They, like me, feel that it is a kind of surrender. An admission that we have lost the battle. They prefer to pretend that Owen never existed in the first place.

If Owen isn't real, if they never held his tiny, newborn body in the curve of their arm, if they never watched in pride as he ripped through his pile of carefully wrapped birthday presents, if they hadn't ever pinched his cheeks and told him he would grow up to be strong and brave, just like his Nonno, then they couldn't possibly feel the soul-crushing pain of losing him. They don't speak his name. They don't acknowledge that I gave birth or raised a child for almost five years or am still, even without my child, a mother.

As Italian immigrants, they still hold onto a lot of old-country ideas. They doted on Owen, much more so than his older girl cousins, burying him in gifts and food and compliments. They started a college fund before he could even walk and wall-papered their home with his photos. To them, he would be the future head of the family, after both they and Geneva failed to produce a son. The one cushion to the blow of their sinful youngest daughter giving birth outside of marriage was that my son would carry on the Lazzari name. But now that he is gone, the photos have mostly come down, and their focus has swung back to Geneva's girls, Mikayla and Audrey. They are the center of all of my parents' adoration.

My mother and father would be mortified to hear that I see a therapist. I try picturing them sitting on the sand-colored couch in Jane's office, surrounded by her soothing art and hand-embroidered throw pillows, as they casually talk about their feelings in their softly accented voices. The image doesn't work. It would be impossible for them to understand laying out all of your dirty laundry in front of a stranger. Lazzari family secrets are guarded fiercely. Alcoholic uncle? He's "high spirited." Cousin got booted from UConn after she failed every class in her first semester? She's "taking some time off." Their daughter allowed her son to go missing from her own house? Well, that one's a little harder to keep quiet. Even so, the topic is avoided at pretty much all costs. They ask about my job, my husband, my somehow always disappointing cooking–but never anything potentially deeper than that. Even then, they shake their heads at the answers, make the sign of the cross, and silently ask Jesus to help me pull my shit together.

As usual, they won't be at the benefit tonight, which is a small miracle. I don't need any more fuel on the fire of this hellish week. It's the last thing I want to do at the moment, but somehow Geneva had manipulated a promise of attendance out of me several weeks earlier. *This is a big one, Ellie, you know that*, she had said, her eyes filling with tears. *Two years*, she said dramatically. As if I didn't know.

I don't remember which charity is benefiting from tonight's event, but Geneva has told me that there will be an extended remembrance for Owen, being his anniversary and all. The usual one, that Geneva uses to kick off all of her events, is relatively brief. But tonight, I expect she will have more photos projected up on the big screen, more facts about his life—like his love of superheroes and Legos—the details of his disappearance, a plea for everyone to keep him in their hearts and prayers, and, of course, to keep looking for him. She might even have one of her girls in their pre-teen awkwardness come up and talk about their little cousin and how much they miss him. Good Lord, do I not want to go.

When Daniel walks in the door just after five, I'm still sitting in the kitchen. There are dishes in the sink, a pile of unopened mail on the table, my purse and shoes on the floor. I watch his eyes sweep around the room, taking in the chaos and me, still in my work clothes, sitting in the near-dark. He flips on the light and sits in the chair across from mine. His face is impossible to read.

"Alright?" he asks.

I say nothing.

"Were there reporters here?" he asks. I shake my head. He frowns. "Huh. I'm surprised." I look away.

"We have the benefit," I say, my voice thick.

"I know. We don't have to go." He is no more impressed with Geneva's efforts than I am.

"We have to. It's…" The words stop in my throat. He closes a warm hand over mine. I turn to look at his handsome face. *He really is a good man*, I think to myself. I don't deserve him.

"Ok," he says.

We both get up and start for the bedroom to get changed. I go back to grab my discarded shoes, which are by the counter where the house phone sits. As I bend down to get them, I notice a red light blinking on the side of the phone. I look closer. Above the light, it says, VOICEMAIL. And the light is blinking under the OFF button. I can hear Daniel walking around the bedroom upstairs.

Son of a bitch.

CHAPTER 7

We make it to the benefit after a silent car ride. I'd thrown on a loose black dress, leggings, and tall boots that are barely formal enough for the event, which is being hosted at the Museum of Fine Arts in Boston. Geneva's face tightens when she sees me, but then flashes into her *ON* smile. She strides across the lobby, her impressively high heels attacking the floor with each step. She looks perfect. Dark hair pulled back in a dancer's knot at the back of her head, pearl necklace sitting at the base of her throat, a gorgeous ruby colored dress wrapping her slim figure and tied elegantly at her waist in some kind of intricate knot. She's even wearing legit pantyhose. I didn't think people wore those anymore. But somehow she makes them look good.

Geneva pins a white rose corsage with a blue ribbon on my dress. It looks idiotic to me, but she assures me in a quiet but firm whisper that it's appropriate. She takes my arm and guides me out to the Atrium, where the reception is being held, and introduces me to an endless number of seemingly important people. I instantly forget their names. I have no mind for recording new information like this. They are all Susan or James or Clare or Eddie, and they are all SO honored to meet me. Each one shakes my hand for a moment too long. Half of them hold unwavering eye contact, almost trying to prove that they are comfortable and supportive around someone like me. The other half look at my forehead, or just over my shoulder, or carefully examine my ridiculous corsage. Maybe they think they'll catch my bad luck if they look me in the eye.

After a dozen pointless and painful conversations, I finally break away. Daniel finds me just as I make my way over to the bartender. Without asking, he steps in and hands me a club soda with a lime. Does he know about my liquid lunch, somehow? I try to decide if he is being protective or judgmental. It's so hard to tell sometimes. I see he has helped himself to a whiskey. I can't stand the smell and turn away.

Scanning the room, I notice my nieces sitting at a small table with my brother-in-law. He gets up and gives me a quick kiss on the cheek when we walk over. Nathan is very tall and exceedingly good at handling Geneva's Type A tendencies. He and Daniel shake hands, and I squeeze Mikayla and Audrey in tight hugs. I pull a chair up in between them so that our knees are all sandwiched together. Audrey immediately puts her head on my shoulder.

"Bored yet?" I whisper to them. I can feel her smile against my shoulder, and Mikayla giggles. I love these girls to death. Despite being raised by my high-strung sister, they are sweet, caring people whose quiet maturity lets them generally fly under the radar of Genny's helicoptering. They have their father's patience and Geneva's glossy black hair, which they both wear straight down to their waists. Their wrists are full of bracelets that say things like "She Knew She Could, So She Did," "Girl Boss," and "Fearless." They are both far cooler than I ever was.

"We don't mind," Mikayla assures me but I know they would rather be anywhere else. At twelve and thirteen, their lives are full of intricate friendships, unstable social rules, and apps on their iPhones that I can't even begin to comprehend. These events must be torture for them.

"You say that now," I tease her. "But the boring part hasn't even started."

The rest of the night is as tedious as expected. There are a few reporters here, but they don't approach me, which is surprising. When I point this out to Daniel, he rolls his eyes.

"Small favors, right?" he asks. As if I should be grateful that no one is thinking about Owen anymore. No one is wondering where he is. No one is looking for him. My stomach pinches in pain even though I know it isn't what he meant.

After a respectable but tortuous amount of time, we finally slip out and manage another wordless car ride home. I can't decide whether to ask Daniel about the phone. He must have turned off the voicemail, thinking he was saving me from something. Instead, it feels like he's shutting Owen out. Denying my memory of him. It makes me want to scream at him. Beat on his chest like a crazy person. Shove Owen's picture in his face and shout his name over and over. But I'm so tired. So I say nothing and stare out of the car window at the trees and houses and cars streaming by. And scream inside of my head instead.

When I get to my therapy appointment the following week I still don't feel like talking. I think Jane understands. She talks at me for a while, including some long pauses, leaving plenty of room for me to jump in. But I can barely manage more than a few nods and shrugs. Even her floral jumpsuit and red leather boots don't stir up much of a reaction in me.

I wonder if I'm actually dead inside, if there are pieces of me that no longer exist. People talk about their hearts walking around outside of their bodies once they have children. And yes, I have spent the last two years missing an essential part of who I am. But it didn't end there. I started with an Owen-shaped hole inside of me that was left smoldering and it has slowly burned away more and more until there's almost nothing left, just the curling brittle edges like a singed piece of paper.

This is all going on in my head while Jane studies me. She doesn't push. Instead, she seems to know when to go forward and when to pull back—a skill that so many others lack. I don't like being around people all that much for exactly this reason. The questions, the lack of boundaries, the sharing of personal space. It's suffocating.

A few years before Owen was born, some friends and I went to a Kenny Chesney concert at Gillette Stadium. Picture sixty-five thousand drunk people in cowboy hats. The concert itself wasn't so bad, aside from the lines for the ladies' room stretching all the way across the concourse. But after the show ended, everyone tried to leave at once. People funneled out to the parking lots in a giant wave—a great mass of bodies, still shouting and singing and cheering, falling over each other, banging into people, creating a forward-moving swarm of chaos.

My friends and I bunched together, linking arms to keep in contact. At one point, outside the stadium, we had to stop at a busy crosswalk that stretched across a four-lane road. A police officer directed the crowd, making us pause to let cars go by. With thousands of concert-goers behind us still surging forward, not seeing the obstruction up ahead, we were pressed into the backs of the people ahead of us.

Overwhelmed by the scent of sweat, body odor, vomit, and alcohol, and the pressure of tons of bodies, I suddenly couldn't breathe. Panic tore through me in a hot flash, and I swayed against the man standing behind me. He gently pushed me back toward my friends, probably assuming I was too drunk to stand. I couldn't draw in a clean breath of air.

I turned to my nearest friend, who still had her arm linked with mine, but I couldn't see her. My vision had zoomed down to two tiny pin pricks of light. I tried to tell her I was going to pass out, but I couldn't hear myself speak. Ahead, the officer waved the crowd forward and we started moving. I stumbled across the street and somehow made it back to our car, shaking and crying. I couldn't explain to my friends exactly what happened. They propped me up in the back seat and took me home, thinking the night had gotten the better of me.

By the next day, I had shaken it off, assuming it was a one-time thing and that I likely had one drink too many or gotten over-heated in the crowd. But more and more, I feel that sense of panic when people are around me. I always have the fear that there is something they want from me, even if I'm in a crowd of strangers. I know I'll fail — that the people will push against me, forcing me to one side or the other, pressing for something I can't give. The guests at a benefit. My coworkers. People who squint at me at the grocery store, trying to figure out where they've seen my face before. My family. Daniel.

"I let all of them down," I tell Jane. She waits. She wants more from me too. Just like everyone else. A tear slips out. It must be my billionth. Or trillionth. They are unending. One after the other. Pieces of my soul, slowly leaking away. I am so used to them that I don't wipe this one away. It makes a slow trek down my cheek, and then down my neck to eventually absorb into the collar of my shirt. Jane waits for it to complete its journey.

"Is that why you've stopped trying?" she asks. "Because you assume that you'll fail?"

This seems fairly obvious to me. I try, but I can't think of a single thing in my life that I am doing well. I draw in a ragged breath, trying to put into words just how much of a failure I know myself to be. But the words don't come. Only tears. And with a quick hug and a handful of tissues, Jane ends our session for the day.

I don't remember calling the police. But suddenly they are there, blue lights flashing in the darkness. I've already run up and down the street calling his name, then back behind our shed and through the hedges into the neighbors' backyards on both sides of us. I find nothing.

No sign of him. No little green sock. No stuffed Spiderman. Nothing. An officer catches me in his arms as I run back into the house, frantic and hysterical. He forces me to sit in a kitchen chair and describe what happened. I tell him I put Owen to bed, like always. I tell him I went to take a shower, like always, and checked on him, LIKE ALWAYS. But he wasn't there, he was gone. But I've already told him that, haven't I? Why doesn't he understand?

I can't sit still. The longer he makes me sit there, the further away Owen gets – I can feel it. I'm begging him to help. To go look for my baby. He assures me that people are already out looking, that they are doing their best.

You don't even know what he looks like, I shriek into his young, clean-shaven face. His badge says Campbell.

Officer Campbell watches as I yank open the drawer where I keep the few pictures I've actually bothered to print and start tearing through them. The most recent ones are already months old. His face is there – Owen's face that looks so much like mine – over and over, but they aren't right. They don't show him exactly the way he looks now. This one of him on the swing set behind my parent's house doesn't catch the color of his eyes. This one where he's laughing makes him look younger than his almost five years. In this one of him squeezed on the couch between his cousins, his face is turned so you can't see his sweet smile. How will they know what to look for? I shove all the pictures at Officer Campbell, insisting that he take them, search them, learn them. Know my baby's face so he can bring him home to me.

CHAPTER 8

I spend the next two weeks in bed. I can't eat. I don't want to talk to anyone. I get up long enough to make Daniel his coffee, turning my face away from the smell. I wait for his car to pull out of the driveway before I climb back in bed and drop into unconsciousness—the one place I can get away from my own thoughts. When I do wake up, I run through the numbers. Two years. Twenty-four months. 733 days. Then, 734. Then, 735. Each morning, another tally mark in the days-without-my-child column. I cry until I'm so dehydrated that nothing comes out anymore. I ignore my phone. I don't turn on the TV or the radio or my laptop. I pull the curtains and don't turn on the lights. I let the darkness pool around me, filling in all the empty space around my bed until I feel embraced by it. Darkness around me, darkness inside of me.

I close my eyes and let myself drift far away, to a different world, a different life. One where I haven't screwed up everything I've ever tried to do. One where nothing is ever lost, where grief doesn't exist. Where this massive, grinding weight I carry around with me all the time is lifted off and I can stand up straight for the first time in I don't know how long. I can take a full breath, all the way down into my lungs, filling me up with clean air, and the tightness that always crushes my chest is gone, like someone has cut the cord that has been squeezing the life out of me.

And then, suddenly, like I'm thrown down an open tunnel, I plunge back into reality when I wake up and remember that the worst is true. The weight is still there, along with the grief, the pain and the debilitating constriction that doesn't let me breathe. Then I get mad at myself for giving in, for giving up. Nothing I'm doing is helping anyone, let alone Owen. The darkness can't hide the piles of laundry I haven't touched or the requests for overdue reports for work that I'm sure are stacking up in my inbox. It's all there waiting, reminding me of everything I haven't done or don't do. But I can't work up the energy to do anything about it. Sleep is so much easier.

On the following Friday evening, I force myself to take a shower and change into clean clothes. I make the bed and wait for Daniel to get home. He hasn't said anything about my behavior these past two weeks. Just thanked me for his coffee and ignored the fact that he hasn't seen me in real clothes in days. I'm sure he doesn't know what to do with me — like I'm some sort of wild animal who may startle if he moves too quickly. We do a lot of literal and physical tip-toeing these days. I'm honestly surprised he keeps coming home every night but it's comforting to know that he will. Predictability is a good thing. Though at the same time, I also dread his arrival. He's the one person I actually have to answer to. He's the one who will judge me if I stay in bed all day, which is why I at least put on the show of coffee-making in the mornings. But I know he's not falling for it.

I am contemplating making dinner. It's the least I could do, though the fridge is mostly empty. I wonder what Daniel has been eating all week. I hate cooking. My mother considers this another of my huge disappointments. She would spend all day making a pot of sauce — something that sounds vaguely torturous to me. But I usually at least try to make something before Daniel gets home. As I'm standing in the kitchen, trying to get my act together, I get a text message from Anton. I read it, ignoring the multiple messages and missed calls from Geneva and my mother.

"Hellooo??? Earth to Ellie!" Anton says.

"??" I answer.

"When's the last time you checked your email??" he asks.

Shit, I think. I've completely checked out.

"What's up?" I text, as I try to power on my laptop. The battery is completely dead. I dig through my bag, looking for the power cord.

"READ THE EMAIL," Anton texts back. By the time my computer turns on, I'm in a full panic. There are hundreds of emails in my inbox, and my stomach drops, wondering how much I've missed. I click through them, looking for the bad news, since I assume that's what Anton means.

"*Instant Progressive Web Apps*"

"*Promote your business with professional printing!*"

"*Canceled: Meeting: 9AM Conference call for Finance team*"

"*Reminder – Monthly sales reports due for all reps*"

"*Register now! Account-based sales webinar*"

I click Delete on each of them until I find one from Barry. The subject reads: *My deepest thanks*. It's a goodbye letter to the company, thanking everyone for ten happy and profitable years.

"With the recent changes, it has come time for me to find my next adventure," it says. I text Anton.

"At least he didn't say journey."

"LOL" he replies.

"What's everyone saying?"

"That there's probably more coming."

There is. After I text Daniel, asking him to pick up sushi for dinner on his way home, I dig through to the bottom of my inbox, where I find an email from Flavia asking me to come in on Monday afternoon. She doesn't mention what the meeting is about, but between the acquisition and Barry's departure, I assume the worst.

I spend the weekend catching up on all of my overdue work. I answer every email in my inbox, follow up on every request. Daniel moves around me, not saying much. He tries to get me to eat, but I still have no appetite. He fills glasses of water and puts a straw in my mouth, forcing me to drink. I do it to make him go away, taking a few sips to ease his conscience, barely looking away from the computer screen. He speaks to me, but I don't hear him. He pulls me into the bedroom at night, trying to get me to sleep, but I bring my laptop and work through the night. I feel a frantic need to prove my worth to Flavia before Monday, and I know I don't have much time. I work until my eyes are bloodshot and dry.

Finally, late on Sunday night, I can't stay awake any longer. I fall into a fitful sleep around midnight and dream that I'm trying to walk along the roof line of our house. The shingles are slippery and crumbling and the empty air sucks at me, pulling me to either side. I know no matter which way I lean, or how hard I try to keep my balance, I will inevitably fall.

Flavia and the human resources manager, Tonya, are waiting for me when I get to Flavia's office, their faces solemn. I want to make a joke about saving them some time and just calling it quits, but I don't. Suddenly my herculean efforts to get my work done over the weekend seem ridiculous. I wonder what the hell I was thinking and I have to stop myself from laughing. I know what's coming. I knew it as soon as I saw Flavia's email. Daniel's face flashes through my mind. He'll be furious, I know. I realize that my last-ditch effort has been for him, to show him I was trying to keep my job. Major fail, as my nieces would say.

I sit in the chair they have pulled out for me. On the desk there are two folders — one orange and one blue — that both have a white sticker on the front with ELEANORA LAZZARI printed on them. I listen as they explain about staffing redundancies and streamlining efforts and how, even though I've done a fine job, there's just no need for an under-trained, unreliable analyst. They don't actually say the under-trained and unreliable part, but I go ahead and mentally fill it in for them. I want to tell them it's ok, that they don't need to try to make me feel better. But they are on a roll, so I let them say what they brought me in to hear. I'm about to reach into my bag to hand over my laptop and security badge when Flavia says something I'm not expecting.

"Ellie, this," she says, pointing to the orange folder, "is your severance agreement and COBRA information."

"This one," she points to the blue folder, "is a job offer." I raise my eyebrows.

"You were one of the best salespeople on the team," she says. "You were consistent and motivated, and I could always rely on you to hit your numbers. You are the kind of person we still want around here as we move forward with combining the teams. So, if you are willing to step back into that role, then we would be happy to have you. And," she adds, glancing at Tonya, "I have talked HR into offering you a Director-level compensation package." Flavia clearly thinks this is a big deal. Her face is so hopeful that I almost, *almost* reach out to open the blue folder and see what the numbers look like. She sees me hesitate.

"I know the past few years have been terrible for you. No one is denying that. And I'm glad that we've been able to keep you on board this long. But I would love to see you get back to what you used to love doing." She leans in, almost begging, telling me that there is this other person who used to exist, who had good qualities, who no one has seen in a very long time.

I want to hug her and run away at the same time.

I think back to being that person. She was quick on her feet. She was thorough and detailed. She knew where to go and what to say. She wore mascara and never thought to check if it was waterproof. All the parts of her brain worked together at once. Sentences came out in the right order. She wore high heels and shook hands and remembered names when people introduced themselves. She might not have been perfect all the time, might not have always made the best decisions, but in general, she could hold her own. Right now, I wouldn't recognize that person if she was sitting next to me in this office.

I politely decline their offer and accept the orange folder. I don't have a desk, so I don't need to dramatically carry a cardboard box of my things out to my car. But I walk through the office to say goodbye to Anton only to find his desk is empty and his name tag already removed. Another sales guy named Randy tells me he was one of the first to go earlier that morning.

"It's been a fucking witch hunt around here," he says, before scurrying back to his cubicle. I look around. Everyone is huddled at their desk, pounding away at their keyboards, determined to look busy and important. There are half a dozen empty desks around Anton's. I can see Ellen in the marketing department pulling pictures off of her cubicle walls, tears running down her face. I'm filled with relief that I won't have to come back.

I text Anton from the parking lot.

"☹"

"You too?" he asks.

"Uh huh. Where r u?"

"Out celebrating. Get your ass over here. I'll order one for you"

He's at the same bar where we had gin and tonics a few weeks ago. He hops off of his bar stool and gives me a quick hug when I walk in.

"I get why they canned me, but why you?" I ask, as we clink glasses in a mock toast.

"Eh," he says. "I was never any good." I mildly protest, but we both know it's true. Anton is a sweetheart. One who is far too human to have the killer instinct needed for sales. "I was scraping by, hoping nobody noticed how much I sucked at selling things."

"What are you going to do now?" He shrugs.

"I'll figure something out. I've got to be better at something than this."

He smiles his sweet smile, and I genuinely feel bad for him. He runs a hand over his almost bare head. When I had last seen him Anton had been hanging on to the last of his hair, hoping, it seemed, that it would make a difference. But sometime in the last few weeks he had apparently taken the plunge and shaved his head clean. It looks better, like he is choosing a buzz cut rather than living with going bald. My heart warms for him, knowing it must have killed him to cut off the little hair he had left.

We toss around a few career ideas as we finish our drinks and order another round. My stomach is empty, so halfway through the second one, I already feel woozy. We do a round of "remember when" and recall some horror stories from our worst customers.

"Six months of kissing that guy's ass and all I get was a *'Sorry, but we'll have to pass!'*" Anton laughs. "Waste of fucking time."

"Well, you won't have to do that anymore," I say, trying to sound positive, but I'm pretty tipsy, so it comes out with a giggle. He playfully punches my arm.

"What about you?" he asks, his tone growing more serious. He knows it's a loaded question.

"I don't care!" I say with false bravado, not looking him in the eye. "What does it matter? I sucked at this. I'm sure I'll find something else to suck at."

"What will Daniel say?" he asks.

But I don't want to think about the answer, so I ask him how his love life is going.

"Different girl every night, lucky if I remember their name in the morning," he jokes. "It's a sweet life—no one to answer to, no one tying me down."

I squeeze his hand, and he gives me a sad smile. I know he has had a history of bad luck with dating and that he wants nothing more than to find someone.

"Ellie," he asks, his eyes glazed over with alcohol, "can I ask you something?"

I stiffen a little. People only say that when they want to ask about Owen. I nod.

"Are you and Daniel happy?" he asks. Not the question I was expecting. The answer is obviously no, no we aren't happy because I'm not happy. Because I don't know what happy is anymore.

"It's complicated." I look down into my glass of melting ice.

"Because of Owen?" he asks. There it is — his name like a little punch to the gut any time someone else says it. I nod. "Were you happy before…?" He doesn't finish the question. He doesn't have to.

"Of course," I answer quickly. A little too quickly. I drain the last few drops of my drink. Anton watches me for a minute.

"You know, my sister had a stillborn son," he says, leaning back on his stool. I look back at him.

"I didn't know that."

"Right near the end. Thirty-four, thirty-five weeks, something like that." I cringe, remembering how big I had been with Owen by that time. "They thought they were in the clear. She had four miscarriages before she got pregnant with her son. They all ended very early, but with the fifth one, they made it past the point where they thought they had to worry. They waited until she was pretty far along to tell anyone. But they eventually got wrapped up in it and decorated his room, bought a bunch of baby stuff," he tells me. His face is drawn, and I can feel his sadness. I don't want to hear the end of the story.

"They even named him. Marcus," he says. "After my dad." I take his hand in mine. I'm finding it hard to draw in a full breath. "Everything seemed fine. And then, Emily went for her regular check-up. The doctor couldn't find his heartbeat. They couldn't figure out what went wrong. Just told her it happens sometimes. She still had to deliver him. She said they let her hold him for as long as she needed to." His eyes are full of tears. I want to stop him, so neither of us has to feel this.

"We had a small funeral. A tiny coffin," he says, wiping his face on a bar napkin. He turns back to me. "That was four years ago. And Emily still talks about him every single day. It doesn't matter that he never took a breath or got to meet his parents or anything. He is a part of her, and she never forgets him."

"Does she have any kids now?" I ask. He nods, smiling.

"She and her husband adopted a little girl last year. Mila." He pulls out his phone to show me a picture of a dimpled, black-haired toddler in pink overalls. He swipes to show the same girl squeezed between two smiling adults. Her adoptive parents, I assume. They are a beautiful family. I smile at him.

"I'm happy for them. And for you," I add.

I feel guilty that I haven't been a good enough friend to know all of this has been going on in Anton's life. I nod to the bartender, who clears away our empty glasses, replacing them with full ones. I take the slice of lime and squeeze it over my drink.

"Ellie," he says.

"Please don't." I know what he wants from me. He wants me to see that there are ways to be happy. That life can go on. But it's different. I don't point out to him that Emily knows exactly where Marcus is, that she got to hold him in her arms before she said goodbye, got to kiss his face and stroke his hair and gently lay him down for the last time. That she can go to sleep every night knowing exactly where he is and how he got there. That she isn't haunted by the knowledge that she failed him when he needed her the most, that she was careless enough to not protect him at his most vulnerable. It's a devastating situation and my heart breaks for Anton and his sister and little baby Marcus. But it doesn't change anything. Anton wraps an arm around my shoulders and leans his head against mine for a minute.

"Ok," he says, and we drop it.

I'm not mad. I know he's just trying to help. I know so many people want to help. But there's nothing they can do. Anton turns back to his phone.

"Let's start job hunting," he says, pulling up a job search website. He clears his throat. "Ok, young lady, what are your qualifications?" he jokes.

Hours later, I wake to an Uber driver telling me to get out of the car. We are in front of my house, but I don't have any memory of getting there. I apologize and stumble out of the car. The porch light comes on, momentarily blinding me, and Daniel comes out to half-carry me into the house. I can't stop giggling.

"I got fired!" I tell him joyfully, stumbling as I kick off my shoes by the front door.

"Laid off," he says shortly. "I know. You texted me hours ago."

"I did? I don't remember doing that."

Daniel doesn't laugh. He doesn't smile. He doesn't kiss me goodnight. He just helps me into bed, and that's the last thing I remember.

CHAPTER 9

I don't hear Daniel leave the next morning. He must have made his own coffee. When I finally manage to peel myself out of bed, desperate for some water, I am still wearing my wrinkled work clothes. My shoes and purse are in a pile by the front door. My coat is next to them, half inside-out from when I yanked it off the night before when I got home. Daniel hasn't bothered to hang it up. There is mail on the kitchen table. Still no food in the fridge. Daniel's dry-cleaned shirts are hanging on the coat rack by the back door, waiting for someone to move them to his closet. I fill a coffee mug with water because there are no clean glasses.

I look around my disheveled house. I can envision myself fixing every one of these things. Cleaning the crumbs from the counter, sweeping the dust bunnies from the corners, taking the trash out to the garage. Each task stacks up in my mind, like a neat pile of bricks. Twenty minutes for dishes, thirty for laundry. Each gets a neat designation of time and effort until I have a clear picture of what my day would be if I handled all of my business like a sensible and productive adult, though, I have to admit, that would just barely be meeting the minimum of grown up responsibilities. I go back to bed.

I set an alarm so I can make it to therapy on time, feeling kind of proud that I've managed that task. But I'm still hungover when I get there and my body aches all over. I've barely eaten for the last week and my insides are kindly reminding me I'm not as young as I used to be. I can't even take a guess at how much I had to drink with Anton, seeing that I can't remember much of the evening. *Clearly too much*, I think to myself, trying to shade my eyes from the lights in Jane's office. They are much brighter than I remember. My voice is hoarse when I tell her what happened the day before.

"I'm sorry to hear that," she says. "Losing your job can feel very personal, like you are losing a piece of yourself. How are you feeling?"

I think about it. But all I'm feeling is nauseous.

"I don't feel anything," I tell her.

"Ok. Sometimes it takes a few days for news like this to sink in," she says.

"No. I get it. They didn't need me. I wasn't doing a good job." I shrug, sending another ripple of pain through my throbbing head. "Makes sense."

"Do you feel a sense of loss?" she asks. I look at her for a long time.

"I... don't feel... anything."

Jane probably thinks I'm stonewalling her. But for the rest of our session, I can't get past the empty feeling. She wants to know if I feel hurt or betrayed. I don't. She wants to know if I feel like I have done something to deserve this, while at the same time assuring me I haven't. But I don't feel that either. I know getting laid off should upset me. Work was one of the few routines I had going, one of the few things that filled up my time and forced me to have to answer to someone. It gave me at least a little sense of purpose. "Maybe I don't need purpose," I tell her.

"Everyone needs to feel purpose in their lives," she says. "Motivation to get up in the morning."

I look up quickly, wondering if she knows how emotionally connected I've been with my bed lately. But her face is open, inviting me to say whatever I want to say. I wonder if she would judge me if I told her I'd robbed a bank that morning. I feel like she wouldn't. She would just ask me why I did it and how I felt about it. For some reason, I find this very annoying. I am so flawed, but she keeps trying to convince me I'm not.

Jane and I go on like this for the next month. She gently pushes; I resist talking. It's not even resistance, though. Simply a void. I have no interest in anything. Food doesn't appeal to me. I don't want to see my family. Daniel and I barely speak. I drift through the days. Sometimes the weekends come and I can't account for all the days of the week passing by. Jane and I are both frustrated, and I consider not going back to see her anymore. But despite our lack of progress, she is a familiar face. One who is always glad, or at least pretends to be glad, to see me. Anyway, I've got nothing else to do and nowhere to go.

One morning after another uncomfortably silent session, my phone rings as I get back into my car. I'm exhausted in every way possible and almost don't answer the phone when I see that it's Geneva. But I've ignored her texts for the last few weeks and, of course, feel terribly guilty about it.

"What's going on?" she asks firmly. This isn't a *what's up* kind of question. She knows things are bad.

"I got laid off," I say.

"Not that. Daniel says you've had a bad couple of weeks."

"He told you that?" I guess I shouldn't be surprised.

"He's been very worried about you," she says. I frown. I can't remember Daniel saying more than two words to me in days.

"I'm fine," I say. But I purposely don't look at my reflection in the rearview mirror. I know what I'll see. Sunken eyes, pale skin, unwashed hair. A mess. Not even a hot mess. Just a goddamned disgusting one.

"Bullshit," she says. "Where are you?" She doesn't wait for me to answer. "Meet me at my house. We'll go out for lunch." It wasn't a question.

She bustles me into her car when I get there and drives us into Boston for lunch. I don't question the distance. I let her take over, and, in a way, I'm grateful. I don't question why she isn't at work either. I know why. I realize just how worried she must be.

"This is my new favorite place for lunch," she says cheerfully, when we park in the Seaport, walk down a short side street and stop at a brick building that holds a restaurant I've never heard of. The hostess recognizes my sister, greeting her by name and brings us to a small table in the corner, where Geneva immediately drops the chipper tone. She takes the drinks menu out of my hand and orders us both green tea with lemon.

"Ellie, something has to change," she says, reaching across the table and grabbing my hand.

Her nails are perfectly manicured pink ovals, shiny and smooth. They complement her long fingers and enormous diamond rings, like one of those old Palmolive ads. My own engagement ring is an emerald in an Art Deco style setting. I remember looking through the window of a jewelry store with Daniel, pointing out how common and cold the diamonds looked. They seemed so generic to me. He had tucked that information away and proposed with a vintage emerald ring he had found at an antique dealer. Right now, it's digging into my skin under Genny's gripping fingers. I pull my hand away, and she looks hurt.

"Daniel tells me you are still seeing a therapist," she probes. "That's great. Do you think it's helping?"

"It's not hurting," I say, trying to smile a bit.

"Well, not getting out of bed for days at a time is not normal," she says. "The apathy, losing your job, avoiding people, the drinking…"

I frown. *Is Daniel telling people I'm drinking?*

"Give me a break, Genny. You don't need to baby me. I am fine." *How many times have I had to say that?*

"You realize Nathan had to drive your car home the night you got laid off, right?" she asks. I look blankly back at her.

Shit, I think. I hadn't even thought about how my car made it back to our house. My face burns red. I mumble an apology as the waiter comes to take our order. I don't even look up so Genny orders for both of us. She looks back at me and sighs.

"Look, Ellie, we've talked about this a million times. You will never get over losing Owen. No one expects you to. But you are young. You have so much of your life left. You have to figure out a way to move forward—not move on," she adds before I can protest. "But figure out what the rest of your life is about. You have a great husband who loves you. You are smart and resourceful. You have everything you need to make a good life for yourself. I know it's not the life you thought you would have with Owen, but it can still be a good one. You can still find some kind of happiness—something that brings you some joy, whether that is a new job, a hobby, working with the foundation, whatever. Just something good in your life. Because, if I'm being honest with you, you are giving up, letting the worst of your thoughts take over and keep you down. Do you know what I mean?" she asks.

But I'm not listening. I'm not seeing her concerned face or hearing her speak the exact truth that I am so afraid people will know about me. I can't respond to her question because, as if she has conjured him up with just her words, I can see Daniel. Daniel, who probably thinks that I am still buried in piles of unwashed laundry, unconscious in our bed under the blue striped duvet we picked out at Pottery Barn and paid way too much for because he was trying to cheer me up, surrounded by pictures of us on the tiny honeymoon we took to Martha's Vineyard and the ones of Owen's drooling baby face, hung on the walls of our house. He probably assumes I haven't showered or even vaguely considered doing anything social. He most likely doesn't remember that Tuesdays are therapy days, meaning I have a good reason to be out of the house. He certainly doesn't think it's likely that I have driven all the way into the city, not even realizing that Geneva's new favorite place to get lunch is only a few blocks from his office.

But, as karma would have it, here I am on the other side of the restaurant from where he is sitting at the bar. And in an almost comically slow-motion gesture, he puts his hand on the leg of the woman next to him. Not tapping her on the knee, asking to pass the menu. Not playfully patting the leg of an old friend as he tells her a joke. Instead, he is sliding his hand high up on her thigh as she leans in and smiles at him. But just as he does this, this intimate, flirty, unmistakable thing, his head turns and his eyes, the gorgeous green eyes that I fell in love with not that long ago, land on me, and the smile drops so suddenly from his face that the woman whips her head around to see what has so greatly shocked him, and he pulls his hand back like her leg is on fire.

I can only imagine what they both see. One gorgeous, tall, polished sister, with her whole life neatly tied up in a bow, and me—red-eyed, dull-haired, open-mouthed disaster. Genny turns to see what I'm staring at, and it's such a funny picture—them seeing us and us seeing them—that I laugh. I laugh and laugh and laugh until everyone in the restaurant turns and stares. Genny grabs my arm and pulls me out of there, away from him, away from the woman, away from the perfectly arranged avocado and arugula salads the waiter has just brought to our table.

Back outside, walking quickly toward the car, Geneva's hand still on my arm propelling me forward, my laughter turned sour in my throat, I feel regret. I'm pretty sure I've ruined her favorite lunch place.

CHAPTER 10

Daniel is having an affair. Not a flirty lunch or a first date. A relationship. He has feelings for her, she has feelings for him, blah, blah, blah. How adorable. He comes home that night to explain all of this to me. I sit and listen, letting him say his piece. I don't argue when he packs a small bag and tells me he needs some space, some time to think, and leaves our house. Except it's not really our house. It never has been. It's mine and Owen's. Daniel can leave it all he wants. He can take his records and his shirts and his coffee maker and leave and never feel one thing about it. But I can never leave. Because Owen is here, even if he isn't really.

I sit on our living room couch after Daniel leaves, looking at the disaster that I have allowed to grow around me. In Owen's house. In his space. In the places his toys and books and baby blankets used to be. My stomach tightens into a knot and starts to shake. I can feel it vibrate inside of me, buzzing around until my whole body is shaking. I've let him down. I've failed him.

So, for five days straight, I clean. The stacks of dishes, the dust, the dirty sheets, the clothes and shoes that have piled in corners — all of it. But once it's done, it still doesn't feel right. So, I disinfect every surface, wash every window, even get the ladder out of the garage and wash them from the outside. I take everything out of the fridge and scrub every dried-on stain or spill, and then throw away everything that is even coming close to the expiration date. I take down all the curtains, wash them, iron them, and hang them back up. I rent a carpet shampooer and wash the carpets, then leave the windows and doors open for two days so they will dry, even though it's only forty degrees out. I empty, wipe down, and reorganize every cabinet. I throw out grocery fliers and chargers to phones we don't own anymore and socks with holes in them. I purge and scrub and scrape, stopping only when I feel so faint that I am almost unconscious on my feet. I choke down a few bites of food, living on pretzels and spoonfuls of peanut butter and half a jar of olives. Those things never go bad.

I put Daniel's shirts away and wash his dirty laundry. I neaten the sweaters on his shelves and wipe the bits of his hair from the sink from when he shaved on Tuesday morning. I file away bills with his name on them and recycle his old magazines. I pile up the pillows on his side of the bed as if everything is just fine. I don't open his drawers or look through the pockets of his jackets or search through the credit card statement, line by line, looking for evidence to use against him. I move around and in his space as if he is coming back very soon, whether that is true or not.

Geneva stops by a few times to check on me when I don't answer my phone. She tries to get me to talk about Daniel as she follows me around the house, but I can't see the point.

"He's going to do what he wants to do," I tell her. I get it. I was a shit wife, and he needed something better. Her eyes fill with tears when I say this, but I'm too busy organizing the linen closet, getting the edge of every towel to perfectly line up in an exact row, to stop and comfort her. She feels horribly guilty about the restaurant, as if my husband's infidelity is her fault. But we all know who to blame. I keep cleaning.

On Sunday afternoon, she appears again, armed with Mikayla and Audrey and a bag of groceries that she swiftly puts away on the empty shelves. When I see the girls, I stop what I'm doing and hug them tightly. I am instantly aware of how crazy I must look and feel horrible that they have to see me like this. Audrey wrinkles her nose.

"What's that smell?" she asks.

"It's bleach," Geneva answers. She opens the window in the kitchen and waves her hands, trying to clear the air. She puts the cap back on the bottle of bleach that I had been using to clean the sink.

"Enough of that," she says, tucking the bottle back under the sink. "Girls," she says sternly to the three of us, "we are going to Nonna's house for dinner. Aunt Ellie needs some help getting ready." The girls smile and push me toward the bathroom.

After I get most of my protestations out of the way, I let them draw me a bath and look the other way when they dump in six different flavors of bath salts. They leave me alone in the bathroom to get in while heading off to find me something "awesome" to wear.

"Pick something that Nonna will like!" I call after them, hating myself for even thinking such a thing, knowing that no matter what, my mother will find fault with my clothes, my hair, with me. I haven't spoken to her in weeks and I don't know what Geneva has told her—probably too much. I don't even want to think about it.

My legs shake as I lower my body into the bath. My hands are already water-logged from the barrage of cleaning, my nails all broken and jagged. I study them, half-amazed, half-sad at how old and worn out they look. The water is fragrant and still, and I sink down until it comes to just below my nose, feeling a wash of gratitude for the previous owners of this house for updating the old bathrooms and adding this over-sized soaking tub long before I moved in. I close my eyes to avoid looking at my wavering body under the surface. I had a love/hate relationship with it for a long time but have stopped paying attention to it over the last few years. *Another thing you've given up on*, I can imagine Geneva saying.

I tip my head back so my ears are under the water and I can hear my own heartbeat softly thudding. Without thinking, I steady my breathing until my heart slows. Swirls of hair pool around me, swaying gently in the water. This feels like the first time I've stopped moving in days. The heat makes me woozy. For a moment, I dip all the way under the water, until I feel it meet over the top of my head, soaking the last bit of dry hair. It is close to silent, otherworldly. Without breath, my heartbeat slows even more.

I envision it stopping all together, my body left floating in the water, finally ceasing all movement, all feeling; a release from the disappointment and sadness. My lungs tighten without air, but I hold myself under, completely enveloped in the warmth and quiet. I don't want to leave. My throat burns. *It would be so easy*, I think, *to not come up for air. To just let it all end.* My lungs protest, urging me to breathe. But even that feels like too much effort. Everything takes so much effort these days. Everything is so hard. My head spins and lights burst like fireworks behind my closed eyes, starry and bright. I push my hands against the walls of the bathtub, holding myself under. *Just a few more seconds*, I think.

And then, just like every time, I see my baby. He looks just like me. Dark hair, brown eyes, smooth skin. His face is so clear that I can reach out and cradle his cheek with my hand, like I used to do, brush his thick swatch of hair off of his forehead, kiss his sweet face, and smell his little-boy smell. And for the same reason I can never leave this house, the same reason I always have to answer the phone, the same reason I have refused over and over to hold any kind of funeral or memorial for him, I hoist myself out of the water and gulp in the cold air of the bathroom. Because when Owen comes home, he will need me.

One of the girls knocks on the door a minute later, as I am quietly sobbing in the bathtub, the tears dropping into the bathwater, one by one. Knowing that they are innocently waiting, eager to help me, happy to do this little kindness, inspires me to wash my hair and get out of the tub. I ignore the weeks' worth of stubble growing on my legs. It's winter, after all.

They've picked out dark jeans, a soft gray sweater, and some ankle boots. I had angrily thrown the jeans into the laundry pile weeks ago after trying unsuccessfully to squeeze into them. Today they easily slip over my hips, and the sweater doesn't cling to my stomach. The girls hem and haw over accessories, holding up earrings and necklaces, arguing over which works best with the outfit. They settle on a thin silver necklace studded with sapphire colored crystals and small hoop earrings. I even let them do my hair. Mikayla has been practicing doing blow-outs on her friends, apparently, and tames my hair into a smooth wave that falls softly against my cheek. Audrey gives my makeup a try but gives up in a fit of giggles when she pokes me in the eye with the mascara wand and lets me take over.

By the time we are done, I feel half-human. The makeup has covered the dark circles under my eyes, for the most part, and I take a second to file down the rough edges of my nails.

"Mom, look at her hair!" Mikayla says proudly.

"Thank you, sweetheart," I say. "You did a great job. You could have a career!" Geneva makes a noise that we all pretend not to hear, but I roll my eyes behind her back, making the girls cover up their smiles with their hands. We all load up into Genny's car and head for my parents' house. I take a very, very deep breath and wish urgently for a glass of wine.

The first thing my mother says is that I'm too skinny. We haven't even made it through the door. I want to point out that I couldn't fit into most of my pants a few weeks ago, but I let the comment pass. In all fairness, she ends up telling all four of us that we clearly aren't eating enough and are practically wasting away. Mom takes people's supposed lack of nourishment as a personal insult. I know she will spend the next few hours trying to force as many calories into the lot of us as possible. The house is filled with the smell of the food she has likely spent most of the day cooking. We all kick off our shoes by the front door and gravitate toward the kitchen, where it's about twenty degrees warmer with all the pots bubbling and steaming on the stove. I can feel about two percent of my anxiety fade at this very familiar and comfortable scene.

My parents' house has changed very little in the last thirty years. They don't see any point in doing silly things like updating, redecorating, or modernizing. Because of this, their house has a lot more Formica, linoleum, and wallpaper than you commonly see these days. Lace curtains hang at every window, the table is set with the same green floral Corelle dishes I ate every meal from when I was a kid, and the floor in front of the stove has a worn spot where my mother has stood and worked her magic for so many years.

My dad gives me a quick squeeze and kisses my forehead. He's tall like my sister, so my head rests comfortably on his chest for a moment, my cheek brushing the soft flannel of his shirt. Once a warm brown like mine, his hair is now softened with gray but still lays in a thick wave across his forehead. He's taken to shaving a little less often these days, and spends a great deal of time in his vegetable garden in the warmer months, leaving him with a year-round tan and deep-set lines around his eyes. All of this makes him seem softer around the edges–less like the stern parent I grew up with and more like a cuddly grandpa.

"Come here and give your Nonno a hug!" he says as he pulls away and gathers the girls into a big bear hug, exclaiming about their ever-growing beauty. They blush and smile and make excuses before disappearing back into the living room with their phones in hand.

My mother is too busy with the food, shrugging off the offers of help, to say much else for a while, but I don't get any extra negative vibes from her that would indicate that Geneva has clued her in to what has been going on lately. I watch her cook for a bit while Geneva and Dad chatter at each other in Italian. I've never learned the language, despite my parents speaking it constantly when we were young.

Both Geneva and I went through an agreed-upon rebellious effort to not learn in one of those heart-warming childhood pacts to be nothing like our parents. Where they prayed and preached, we danced to pop music on the radio. When they refused to get cable, we begged to have sleepovers at our friends' houses so we could watch *Friends* and *Saturday Night Live*. We died of embarrassment at their accents and my mom's frumpy clothes and begged her to pack us peanut butter and jelly sandwiches for lunch so we would fit in with our friends. But in the end, Geneva swung back to the other side, embracing our heritage, learning to cook Mom's generation-old recipes, taking her family to church on Sundays, and recently, studying Italian in anticipation of taking the girls to Italy over the summer, not realizing that all her decisions left me alone with our childish mutiny.

Mom announces that dinner will be ready in five minutes, and I instantly flash back to sitting in my old bedroom down the hall. I would throw my homework or magazine or Walkman aside and go to help set the table. Dad would quiz us on our multiplication tables or history facts or whatever it was we were learning in school at that moment. Mom would monitor our intake of food, making sure that everyone was cleaning their plates, and then some. Geneva would rattle on and on about her day or her friends or the A she had gotten on a test or the dance recital she had been rehearsing for.

I would try to compete, but my grades were never quite as good. I'd get straight A's, but Genny would earn them in Honors classes. I would proudly tell them I had just finished reading *Pride and Prejudice* when Genny would chime in that she was reading *War and Peace*, "*Which is obviously WAY longer and more complicated, Ellie-belly. You'll understand it when you're my age.*" I don't think she did it on purpose. I really don't. But somehow, Genny was always just a little bit better.

My mother turns from the stove, pushing a few gray strands of hair back off of her forehead. Her hair was once as dark and shiny as Geneva's. It has thinned quite a bit and now hangs in a little cap around her face, mostly gray with a little black still sprinkled in. She tried, once or twice, to keep up with the other ladies in the neighborhood, styling it into a feathered bob or perming it into a curly mass that she sprayed in place with a magenta can of AquaNet. But after a while, she realized it was better off left to do its own thing, and for years, it hung in a thick smooth curtain down to her shoulders. Only recently she had it trimmed to its current shape and I still can't get used to it.

She takes a deep breath and surveys the kitchen to make sure none of the food preparation has slipped her mind. It hasn't, of course. She could make a meal for thirty people blindfolded without missing a shred of parmesan. Her gaze eventually falls on me, and I mentally brace myself. If it's not my own hair, which has never been as thick or dark as my sister's or mother's, then it will be my clothes or my makeup or my red eyes. She will find something in me that is not living up to the standard she wants for her daughters, something that Genny has managed to do perfectly that I'm falling short on.

My mother's eyes search my face, and I force myself to sit up taller. Her mouth opens to speak, but she says nothing. Instead, she presses her lips back together and softly places her hand on mine in a gesture far gentler than is her normal way. That's when I know that she knows, that Geneva has warned her that I've lost my job and probably lost my husband. That I've spent days or maybe weeks isolating myself away from the rest of the world. That I'm swiftly drowning and can't seem to find my way back to the surface. My eyes burn with tears, and I want to launch myself into her warm arms and let it all go.

But after a few seconds, she pulls her hand back and turns to the oven to heave the massive tray of lasagna out into the world, filling the kitchen with the scent of hot bubbling cheese. The smell hits me full in the face, and despite my sister's exclamation of happiness to see this perfectly crafted meal, despite my father's arm that he has just cast warmly around my shoulders, despite my mother's beaming pride in her own workmanship, despite my beautiful nieces having just appeared in the doorway, lured by the aroma of true, home-cooked Italian food, despite all of that, my body, exhausted, emotional, and running on empty, isn't having it, and I run to the bathroom to be sick.

An hour later, Genny brings me home after dropping the girls off at her own house and puts me to bed. As if I'm a child, she helps me pull off the boots and the soft gray sweater, which she carefully folds and lays on top of the dresser. She takes a cloth and wipes the tears and the makeup off of my face. She pulls back the covers and tucks me in. She brushes the hair off my face and fans it across the pillow. She leans down and hugs me as best she can, considering I'm already curled up in a ball under the blankets. For a second, she rests her forehead against mine.

"I love you," she whispers. And quietly leaves.

CHAPTER 11

I sleep until the next afternoon. Well, first I wake up around six o'clock in the morning, but my house is spotless, my family thinks I'm crazy, my husband is God-knows-where, I don't have a job, and I can't think of one good reason to get out of bed. So, I go back to sleep, and it's after noon when I wake up again. *At least that is one thing I am incredibly good at*, I tell myself. *Points for gold-medal sleeping skills*. I lay in bed for a while, watching the dreary early spring sky through the bedroom window, and let the feelings of guilt really get good and going. I picture both of my parents' faces from the night before when Dad practically had to carry me to Genny's car, and Mikayla's and Audrey's mumbled goodbyes in their driveway. I doubt they will be coming around again soon to help me do my hair.

I surprise myself by wishing that it was Tuesday so I could talk to Jane. I take this as a very good sign, since therapy has always been such a burden, and it hasn't been easy with Jane lately. I don't have a clear idea of what I would even say to her, but I feel like it may just possibly help. I know I need to do better. I sit up and push the covers back, swinging my legs to the side of the bed. They shake when I stand up. I've pushed myself too far this time. Feeling too weak to take a shower, I go to the kitchen and make myself a piece of plain toast and a cup of tea. I have to sit down while the water is boiling and the bread is toasting, but I eventually get everything ready. I sit down and force myself to slowly eat and drink until they are both gone.

Good, I think. *That's very good.* The food settles in my stomach, and I feel a little less woozy. Next, I text Geneva an apology and thank her for the groceries and for taking care of me the night before. She doesn't answer right away, which I'm a little grateful for. Actual two-sided conversations with her can be so exhausting. Then I bear myself up and call my mother to apologize. I tell her it must have been one of those 24-hour stomach bugs because I'm already feeling better.

"Eleanora," she says, her voice thick, "you cannot lie to your own mother. You think I don't know my own child? You are not sick in the stomach; you are sick in the heart."

Her words shock me. She has always been more business than feeling. Her declaration chokes me up, and I can't answer.

"I don't know why you have so much heartache in your life," she continues, softer. "To me, it seems very unfair, but God has a plan for each of us. This isn't the end for you, just like it wasn't the end..." She trails off but I, of course, know what she means. "...before," she eventually finishes. For a moment, I am angry that she won't say his name, but I try to remind myself that she won't say it because it hurts her too badly, not because she doesn't want to think of him.

"I know, Mom," I say, wanting to get off the phone. "Thanks," I add.

"Ok, my dear. No need to be sorry. Please get something to eat, ok?"

"Yes, Mom, I will," I say and hang up. I fight the urge to cry — and the urge to get back in bed. Instead, I close my eyes and spend a few minutes taking deep breaths in and out until my chest isn't tight anymore.

I look around my spotless house. It feels empty, and I wish Daniel was here. Try as I might, I'm not angry at him. Only sad that I haven't been what he needed in a wife. I know I have it in me somewhere. I know how we felt about each other when we were dating and early in our marriage. I wonder if it's possible to find it again. *Hard to do if he never comes home*, the darker part of my mind thinks. I realize I haven't heard a word from him in almost a week. It's a bit more space than I thought he would take. I contemplate texting him, just to say hi, maybe offer an apology to him too, even though I know he owes me a much bigger one. But no, I decide. He asked for space. I'll let him have what he wants for once.

Through sheer determination, I shower and get dressed in real clothes. I go to the store for paper towels and trash bags, since I used them all up in my cleaning spree. I even convince myself to stop at the library and pick out a few books off the front table that always has the bestsellers. A stack of bookmarks sits on the check-out desk. READERS ARE THE BEST ESCAPE ARTISTS, it says. For some reason, that sounds just lovely to me, and I tuck one inside of Jodi Picoult's newest novel.

When I get home, a shopping bag is hanging from my front door knob. Inside is a note from my mother. *For dinner*, it says. There are enough leftovers in the bag for five or six meals. It makes me smile. I manage to eat a little food and read a few chapters. I move slowly and deliberately, focusing on the task in front of me. Food on plate, plate in microwave, press the button, plate on table, fold napkin, one bite, two bites, sip of water. Then, wash fork, wash plate, leftovers in the fridge, and so on. My mind can't wander when I keep it busy, can't replay the bad things that have been plaguing me.

I feel stronger with the food in my stomach. I feel calmer, having apologized to Mom and Geneva. I know the food was a peace offering from Mom. She is clearly worried about me, especially if Geneva has actually told her everything. My sister had texted me while I was at the store, accepting my apology and telling me she'll always be here for me. I know it's true and stop myself from thinking how pathetic I am to need so much help. *Not pathetic*, I try to tell myself. *It's just a rough time. That's all. Everyone needs help sometimes.* But I'm aware that I need it more than most.

I pep-talk myself through the evening and the next morning until my appointment with Jane. We have a lot to talk about, and for the first time in a long time, I find myself ready to speak. So much so that she offers to see me again on Thursday so that we don't have to wait a whole week to keep going.

I tell her about Daniel in a matter-of-fact manner. I tell her about the manic cleaning and the marathon sleeping and the not eating, even though I'm embarrassed to admit it all and can't look her in the eye for a while afterwards. She assures me I'm not crazy, just sad and overwhelmed. I don't tell her about the bathtub because I'm worried she might change her mind about me if I do. I know I should tell her, that it's exactly the reason people go to therapy. But I convince myself we have lots of other stuff we can work on.

We talk about my parents and my sister. She asks me if I know what *inferiority complex* means.

"It means someone who thinks they suck at everything when they really don't," I say.

"Exactly," she says, nodding, her giant gold tassel earrings swaying. "Do you think that might apply to you?"

"No," I say. "Obviously not." She looks puzzled.

"I don't think I suck at everything; I know it," I say. "There is nothing I'm good at, nothing that I've succeeded at."

"Ellie, you know that isn't true. You have a roof over your head, clothes on your back, food in your kitchen. You have a family that loves and cares about you. You have an education, work experience, and the skills to find a new job. These aren't small things. They are excellent building blocks to anchor your life."

I really, really want to argue with her, but it's hard. I want to say that I could easily lose the house and the clothes and the food if Daniel leaves me and I don't get a new job. But I don't. I know she has a point. Just not one that is easy to accept at the moment.

She asks me about eating and points out that I have to take care of myself.

"I know," I answer. "I'm doing the best I can." I mean it.

"Good," she says, sitting back in her chair and smiling at me. "That's all I ever ask of you."

Daniel texts me the following Tuesday, a full two weeks after he left. In a way, it's been easier with him gone. I made up little routines around the house to keep myself moving. They would probably seem insane to anyone else, so I'm glad that he hasn't been around to witness them. I arrange all of my clothes on the bed before I take a shower, laid out like a person with all the pieces in the right places. I set the table—complete with a folded napkin, a knife, spoon, dinner fork, and salad fork, no matter what I am eating, as well as a water glass and a wine glass, even though I haven't drunk at all since the day I got laid off. I wash and dry everything and put them all away after every meal, refusing to use the dishwasher. I iron all of my clothes when they come out of the dryer, regardless of if they need it or not. I am keeping myself busy, making my hands and body move, so my brain can take a rest.

Daniel says that he wants to talk. I feel a quaking deep in my stomach. I'm terrified about what he might say. I know it makes me sound sad and weak, but I don't want him to leave me. I don't want the woman in the restaurant to have him. I want to go backwards in time and do a better job and make it so that he never looked for her in the first place. But I don't know if I will get the chance. Two weeks of silence cannot be a good sign. He tells me he will be home for dinner.

I grab my keys and run to the store to get ingredients to make chicken curry, Daniel's favorite. I can actually cook a half-way decent one, and I love the way it makes the house smell. I feel a tiny spark of happiness, thinking about him and I sitting down to dinner together, and a small flame of hope starts to burn. *I can make this work*, I think. *We will find a way back. I know I've been selfish. I know I've been inconsiderate. I will do better. I will fix us*, I tell myself. On the ride home, I practice what I will say to my husband to convince him we will be ok, that this was just a bump in the road, that we each need the other in our lives, and that I know I can make him happy.

With dinner started, I tear through my closet, searching for the right thing to wear. Daniel has seen me at my absolute worst many times. I'm ashamed, thinking of myself so often unwashed or hung over or wearing the same sweatpants day after day. It's humiliating, and I hope I can find a way to make him forget. Daniel is so put-together, so meticulous. His books are alphabetized on the shelf. His suits hang in color-order in the closet. His shirt is always tucked in.

Trying to blend the neat and organized life Daniel was used to with the chaotic world of raising a child was not always smooth. Owen had only just turned two when he and Daniel met for the first time. In his toddler glory, Owen was covered in crumbs and general stickiness, despite my best effort to present him as the little angel he was to me. Daniel told me in no uncertain terms that he was adorable and sweet. But his toys were always under foot, Goldfish crackers ended up between the couch cushions, and Owen thought it would be fun once or twice to use Daniel's shoes to store the worms he had lovingly gathered from the driveway after it rained. Daniel put on a good face, but I could see his frustration. Kids were too messy, too unpredictable for his taste. He didn't need to tell me he didn't want any more children. That was clear.

But he and Owen did have their moments. Daniel would occasionally read him stories before bed. He didn't do the voices or anything, but Owen never seemed to mind. Or they would walk out to the mailbox together to get the mail. Daniel didn't want Owen running out that close to the street, so he would ask him if he minded a little company. I would see them walking down the driveway, both so particular in their own ways, and I would feel my heart squeeze at the sight of them.

I pull a black and gold lace dress that I wore to my cousin Angela's wedding a few years ago out of the closet. I remember Daniel's face lighting up when he saw me in it. I actually contemplate putting it on, then shove it back in the closet after picturing myself serving up dinner in an evening dress like a lunatic. *Deep breath*. I put on jeans and a loose white blouse with embroidery around the collar. Soft and sweet, I think. Something I would have worn on one of those coffee dates Daniel and I used to have, where we would pick up lattes at the Thinking Cup and walk through Boston Common in the fall—not heading anywhere in particular, just enjoying being together. It seems like a very long time ago.

I've still got another hour before Daniel is supposed to be home. The curry is simmering on the stove, filling the kitchen with its lovely spicy scent. I move around the house, unable to keep still, adjusting picture frames on the wall, fluffing pillows on the couch, and doing half a dozen other things that make absolutely no difference at all. I'm so nervous that I have to go back and swipe on another layer of deodorant. I can't wait to see him but am worried at the same time that this might be the end, that he's giving up on me. I start to rationalize his decision, without knowing whether he's made it or not. *He deserves better. I would do the same thing in his shoes. I've failed him.*

I've pretty much scripted out his whole argument and convinced myself that I can handle it when my phone buzzes on the counter. *It's probably Daniel telling me he's not coming*, I think. Or it's Mom or Geneva checking up on me again. I let it buzz four times before I walk over and make myself look at the screen. *Detective Luzcak*. The whole room spins.

CHAPTER 12

The year that I lost Owen, 33,677 children were reported missing in the United States. It's as if an entire town–a large one–vanished. Most of them are runaways. Most of them are found. Those that are taken are usually taken by a family member or someone who they know. Only the smallest percent are taken by a stranger. An even smaller percent are murdered. Two years after his disappearance, I am no closer to knowing which of those categories my son falls into. I am certain he did not run away. But I don't know who took him, where they took him, or what they did to him.

My wildest hope, the one that I cling to when I go to my darkest places, is that someone desperate to have a child took him for their own. That they have a home for him and have kept him safe, that they had so much love — misguided as it may have been — but they simply lacked a child to place it on. So they took my baby and are raising him the best they can. And that someday, somehow, someone will realize that he is not their baby, that he is my baby, my son, my flesh and blood, and he will come home to me.

All the other possibilities are the ones that I cannot speak of, cannot allow my mind to spend more than two or three seconds on before I start to slide over the edge to insanity. They are the ones that everyone else thinks are most likely now, though no one ever says that to my face. But I can see it in their eyes when they talk about him. They imply he is dead, that he has ceased to be. I know in my soul this isn't true. Something inside of me would know if he was truly gone. My own heart would stop beating, I'm sure of it. If other people want to think that about my child, so be it.

Owen is in the FBI's National Missing and Unidentified Persons registry. All the information surrounding his case is part of the official record, including his height and weight at the time of disappearance, his hair and eye color, his blood type and what he was wearing when last seen. Whenever a child, or the body of a child, is found, their statistics are run against the database and likely matches are returned. Because children grow and change so quickly, because hair and eye color can be altered or disguised, because there are thousands of missing children to check against, identifying these found children can be a challenge. Occasionally, a possible match comes up for Owen. Today is the seventh such occurrence.

Each time it has occurred before, the same thing happens. Detective Luzcak, the detective in charge of Owen's case, calls me. I meet with local police, who show me a picture of a child, or a child's body, and ask me if I think it is my son. All of them have matched his coloring, or close to it. All have appeared to be close to his age and estimated size based on the amount of time passed. None of them have been my son. Luckily, none of these found children have been close enough to me that I have had to see them in person. There has been no dramatic pulling back of a sheet to show me a dead child, like they do on TV. The thought is too horrifying to imagine. A picture is bad enough.

This may all sound very matter of fact, but in reality, the experience is too terrible to illustrate. No words can describe the mix of terror, hope, hesitation, eagerness, and sorrow. If it's a picture of a body, please God don't let him be mine. If it's a living child, please, please let Owen be coming home. And every time, when it's not him, a silent, beseeching prayer that he is still out there somewhere, safe in a stranger's arms.

Then I think, *If someone did take him and keep him, would he remember me?* His captor would have spent two years with him. Did they make him love them? Does he think of them as his family? Does he have a new mother? Worst of all, does he remember me and think I have forgotten him? Does he lay in his bed—*please God let him have a warm bed to sleep in*—and wonder why I don't come and take him home? Maybe he's happy where he is. Maybe he has a brother or sister or a puppy—all things he used to beg me for. Perhaps they tell him I'm dead or that I don't want him anymore. Maybe he believes it.

These thoughts race through my head on the way to the police station. Plus a thousand more. The detective has told me it's a body this time. A boy, estimated to be between six and eight years old. Dark hair, brown eyes. He didn't tell me how the body was found, only that it was somewhere in Nevada. He didn't say how the boy died but that the images are not graphic, though I can't comprehend how a picture of a dead child could not be graphic.

It takes me several long minutes to get out of my car. I panic when I can't find my car keys. My hands are shaking. I dump my purse on the front seat, growing frantic. I'm almost in tears when I realize they are in my coat pocket. I don't even remember putting my coat on at home. An officer is waiting for me when I walk in. Everything is in slow motion. I don't want to go in. My mind is spinning. I wonder if these are the last few moments I have before knowing my baby is dead.

The officer is speaking to me. I can't hear him. I should have called Geneva. *What the hell am I doing*? I shouldn't be here alone. I tell the officer to wait while I text my sister. I can't type the words. I try to say they found a body, that I'm at the police station. My phone keeps correcting *police* to *polite*. I send it anyway because I can't wait any longer. The officer's hand is on my arm. He brings me to a chair at a table in a small room. Another man in a suit joins us. They ask me if I am ready. I'm not. I am. I think I nod to them. They put a folder in front of me. I'm not sure if they want me to open it. I can't make my hands work. Slowly, the officer opens the file and shows me the picture.

I see my child's face. His round cheeks, his tiny nose, his dark hair curling against his forehead. My brain, my heart, my body scream, *No, no, no, no, don't let it be, dear God, please no…* I blink, and he is gone. He was there, in the picture, and then gone when I look again. No, the ears are too big, Owen's were so little and always covered by his hair. There are freckles across this boy's face where Owen has clear golden skin. The boy's eyes are sunken into dark circles. His skin is gray. His lips blue. It's not Owen. It's someone else's baby. Someone else's worst nightmare, and they don't even know it yet. I wonder if there are mothers and fathers in rooms like this across the country looking at this child's face, feeling waves of relief when they realize it's not their child. And one family who will see the picture and know their child will never grow up. Never come home.

I look up to see the officers watching me. I shake my head. No. He's not mine.

"I'm so sorry," I say. I don't say what I'm apologizing for, but they understand. Everyone is sorry.

They close the folder and whisk it away. The man in the suit disappears for a moment and comes back with a box of tissues. They tell me to take as long as I need. I sit in the cold metal chair shaking. My throat is so tight I think it may close up and I will suffocate in that little room. I need to leave.

The officer is waiting outside of the room when I walk out. He looks at me and puts a hand under my arm.

"Will you be able to drive, Miss?" he asks.

I nod again, though I'm pretty sure I can't. I just want to leave there and be in a place where there are no folders of dead children. He helps me to my car and awkwardly pats my shoulder before hurrying back inside. I sit in my car and can't figure out how to turn it on. I can't find my keys again. I cover my face with my hands and sob. I cry for the families in the rooms. For the little boy in the picture. For whoever found that child and had to call the police to report a dead body. For the people whose job it was to pick up his small body, not knowing his name or where he belongs. For the one family whose world is about to end. For the ragged pieces of me that continue to tear away with each new horrible day. For my Owen, who is still out there somewhere. I sob until I'm out of breath and my chest is about to explode, rocking back and forth in the front seat of my car, wishing it would all end.

Suddenly, my car door opens, and Daniel is there. He pulls me out and into his arms. I don't know how he got there, how he knew, but he is there holding me, crushing me against his chest.

"Is it him?" he asks, his voice thick. "Is it him, Ellie?"

But I can't breathe. I can't get the words out. My body racks with sobs, and I cling to him because my legs won't hold me.

"Ellie, please, is it him?" he asks. "Is it Owen? Is it him?" he asks over and over.

I manage to shake my head, and his body almost collapses with relief.

"Thank God," he says. "Thank God, thank God."

Daniel had come home to the pot of curry burning on the stove. He called Genny when I didn't answer, and she told him where I was. She was already on her way, but he told her he would handle it. He tells me all of this when we get back home. He wraps a blanket around my shoulders because I can't stop shivering. We've been through this before. Each time we had done it together. Until this time. This time I've had to do it alone. He sits next to me on the couch.

"Why didn't you call me?" he asks, putting his warm hand on my cold one. "You know I would have been there."

But I didn't know that when I got the call. I don't know if he wants to be here. I tell him this and he hangs his head.

"Ellie, it's confusing," he says with such anguish in his big green eyes that I actually feel bad for him. "But I love you. I've never stopped. And no matter what, I am here for you when you have to deal with this stuff."

It's a nice thought, but it doesn't work like that. Just like the house, Daniel could walk away at any time and be done with it.

"Are you leaving me?" I ask. I don't have the energy to dance around the question.

"No!" His eyes fly open. "At least... I don't think so. I've made some terrible choices lately. But I've ended things with... her."

I wince but am grateful he doesn't say her name. Better if I don't know it. He waits for me to say something but I just look at him.

"I... I am sorry Ellie. You know things have been bad for a long time."

Of course, I know this. And I know the reason. I know it's me, my fault. That's what he means, even though he hasn't said it.

"I don't know if I know how to make it better," I say slowly. "But I want to." My eyes fill with tears for the millionth time.

"Me too," he says and pulls me against him. He has tears in his eyes as well. He takes a deep, shaky breath that I can feel in his chest.

I slip my arms around him, needing to have him close, needing something to lean on. His hands stroke my hair, and I breathe in the clean, woodsy smell of him. I let myself relax, trying to breathe the tension out of me. I'm filled with such intense relief and immense sadness that both feelings war with each other in my brain. I close my eyes and try to make my exhausted, swirling mind go blank. Daniel's hands are running down my back, over and over, so soothing. We haven't touched each other in so long. Not for the first time lately, I long for the times when we could just forget everything but each other, revel in the joy of just feeling good. I haven't felt good in such a goddamned long time. When he bends his head to kiss me, I let him, his mouth covering mine, his breath warm on my face.

We are both swimming in our different desperation, paddling toward each other, trying to stay afloat. We cling to each other with a kind of fierceness and longing, letting all the anger and mourning and disappointment be momentarily forgotten. For the first time in a long time, I don't pull away when he reaches for my body. I close my mind to everything else besides him and let myself go.

CHAPTER 13

Daniel and I are making an effort to fix things. I ask Jane if she does marriage counseling, but she tells me it's not her specialty. She recommends a few colleagues and Daniel and I make an appointment with one of them. I keep my appointments with Jane, though, because I've gotten comfortable with her. I tell her about the picture of the dead boy, and she assures me that the relief I feel is totally normal and does not make me a sociopath — something I have been considering. She likes to remind me I'm normal, that my thoughts and reactions are not completely psycho. She tells me I'm dealing with one of the hardest things a person can go through.

"Unfortunately," she says, "your situation is harder than most because there is no end in sight." As if I don't know. Then she asks me to consider what would change if I was, at some point, able to lay Owen to rest.

My first reaction is that it's a stupid question. What would I do if my son was dead? How can you ask someone that? And he's not dead anyway, so why even think about it? But that isn't what she is asking. She wants me to think about how much I've put on hold since he's been gone. How much life I'm not living. *All of it* seems like a trite answer. She tells me to think about it before our next session.

I go back to making Daniel's coffee. He kisses me goodbye in the morning, a little stiffly at first, but he's trying. He brings me flowers. I can't remember him ever having done this. They are white roses. A white flag. A peace offering. I'm glad they aren't red. Red roses would seem like he was trying too hard. I am hoping we can get back to some basic things like trust and honesty. Romance is still a little too far off to think about.

I make an effort to get up every morning, get dressed, do my hair and makeup. And then a little housecleaning, a trip to the store, read a bit. Daily tasks with beginnings and ends. With Daniel home, I stop the silly rituals but do whatever I can to make our home a place where we both want to be. A few weeks of that, and I'm feeling like we may have a chance.

There are some tense moments. Judith, our marriage counselor, has each of us make a list of things we are sorry for and a list of things we wish the other was sorry for. Other than the affair, I can't think of anything Daniel has done wrong. Part of me wants to say *not loving Owen as much as I do*, but that's not fair. He does love him. How can I expect it to be the same? Judith stops me when I get to the third page of things I'm sorry for. Let's just say, there's a lot of detail. But Daniel isn't looking for an apology for all of it. He just wants me to understand that I've been absent for a long time. He's right, I have, even though I feel like I've had good reasons. He's sorry about the other woman. He says he would undo it if he could, that he had a stupid reaction to feeling lonely and rejected. I believe him, mostly. I still don't know her name and ask him not to say it. He says she's totally forgotten, in the past. I believe him. Mostly.

We also talk about good things. What we used to be, what we want to get back to. We agree we need to dedicate more time to each other, that too much space has grown between us. Daniel says I'm not the same person he married. He's right. One hundred percent. I hardly recognize that woman. Everything that made her interesting or unique has been peeled away, and the part of me that's left is stark and bare and plain. Judith suggests that this doesn't have to be a bad thing. Maybe I can see it as a new beginning, she says. I feel like Jane wouldn't have put it like that, but ok. Maybe.

One afternoon, I get a text from Anton. My stomach does an odd twist when I see his name on my phone, for some reason. I haven't heard from him since our bender the night we got laid off. I guess I'm just embarrassed at how I must have acted, though I can't remember much of it. His message says that he's found a new job. Project manager at a small tech start-up.

"That's a change," I text him. "No more sales?"

"Couldn't do it. Always hated it."

"Happy for you," I say.

"What about u?" he asks.

"Nada."

In all honesty, I haven't even considered looking for a new job. I can't seem to think of any marketable skill that I could offer an employer. I hear Jane's voice in my head asking me what I *want* to do, not what I think I *could* do. *Good question, Jane*, I think. *What* do *I want to do?* But I come up blank on that one too. I'm impressed that Anton has found something different. I wonder how easy that would be.

When I mention Anton's new job to Daniel, he nods politely and asks about my plans. I know things must be financially tight for us. The truth is I made a hell of a lot of money when I worked in sales, which is how I could afford to buy a house in Newton. The analyst job paid far less. Even with Daniel's salary, the mortgage took up a large part of our income. Daniel knows I won't consider selling the house. He's kind enough not to bring it up. But I know money must be a big source of stress for him at the moment. I haven't looked at our bank account in weeks. Selective deniability.

I hate the idea of finding a new job. *So Eleanora, what made you want to leave sales? What's the reason for the gap in your employment?*

I tremble at the thought of a job interview. No one will understand the path I've been down. But still, I will have to try.

Jane agrees it will be good for me.

"You've done a great job lately," she says, nodding. "I see a lot of positive changes. You've come through a hard time these past few months, but I think you would agree that you are moving in the right direction. The time might be right. What do you think?" I frown at her. Taking the hint, she moves on and asks me how things are going with Daniel.

"Pretty good," I say, thinking of the previous weekend. We had gone on a date. Decent clothes. Nice restaurant. We skipped the wine, but the food was good. We held hands in the car. It only felt a little like we were playing parts in a movie, reading our lines. Most of it was ok.

"Do you feel you are getting what you need out of the relationship?" she asks. I frown at her again.

"What do you mean?" I ask.

"Well, every time you mention your husband, you talk about your failings, your shortcomings, the things he needs but isn't getting. But what about him? Does he contribute to the relationship like you are trying to do?"

"He's trying," I tell her. "It's not perfect, but it's getting better."

"Have you asked him for anything?" she pushes, but I don't understand what she's getting at.

"It sounds to me like you are trying your hardest to be what he wants, to fulfill the role that you agreed to when you first got together, and that's fine," she explains. "However, as we've talked about, things have changed since then. Your needs are different than they used to be. He has to be willing to be the supportive, empathetic partner that you need. From what you've told me, you were pretty independent for a long time. It might be hard for you to admit that you need help. It's ok to ask for it. It's not ok to not ask for it and then be upset or distant when you don't get it. He's not a mind reader. Remember to tell him what you need."

Jane's right, of course. I tell her she really should consider the marriage counseling thing. She smiles and assures me that one-on-one is more her style. Then she wraps her fuzzy purple knit poncho more tightly around her and sends me on my way.

On the way home, I can't get her words out of my head. Am I so different that Daniel can't figure out what I need? Have I not told him? Things have been so much better since sleeping together provided the doorway back into our marriage, as silly as that sounds. We haven't done it again, but we are definitely a lot closer than before. It felt wonderful to just let go and be in the moment that night, to just feel physically close to one another and not think about anything else. I didn't want to admit that it was our way back to each other. I mean, we still have a lot of work to do, a lot to figure out. But for that hour, we were right where we both wanted to be.

CHAPTER 14

A few weeks later, when Geneva asks me to go shopping with her and the girls to pick out a dress for Mikayla to wear to her upcoming semi-formal dance, I hesitate. I still feel bad about the girls seeing me at my worst, so much so that I've let a full month go by without seeing them. After everything, I can't imagine that they want me around. But Geneva insists they absolutely need me to be there. She even puts Mikayla on the phone, and, as Geneva knows, I obviously can't say no to her.

They pick me up on Saturday morning when Daniel is at the gym. The girls are in good moods and get into a deep debate about the horrible injustice of their school not allowing girls to wear strapless dresses to the dance.

"I mean, they treat us like children!" Mikayla moans. Audrey nods in emphatic agreement, always willing to go along with her big sister's ideas. Geneva and I catch each other's eye and try not to laugh. We both remember all too well the frustrations of being thirteen.

We head for Nordstrom once we get to the mall, passing by the kids' indoor play area. Toddlers climb the tiny ladders and throw themselves down the plastic slide. Kids clamber over the rainbow-colored structures and run in gleeful circles. Tired parents clutching iced coffees line the ring of benches that are keeping their children contained, making small talk or staring at their phones. Automatically, without thinking, my feet slow and I scan the crowd of little ones, as I do every time there is a gathering of children. My eyes bounce from head to head, looking for the dark waves I know so well. Then, just to be sure, I search each face, looking for his eyes, his little nose. The tiny bodies move in slow motion while I do this inventory, bouncing here and there, each one so unique and dear, each one within arm's distance of their mother or father or grandparent. None of them are my Owen. They never are.

I feel Genny's hand on my arm and turn to see the girls trying not to look at their crazy aunt, who is standing stock still in the middle of the mall, staring at a group of someone else's kids.

"Sorry, I…" I start to say.

"This way!" Geneva says cheerfully, glossing over everyone's discomfort.

Embarrassed, I shake it off and put on a smile, which the girls see and their excitement bounces back to full level as we head into the Nordstrom dress section. The girls immediately attack the racks, holding up dress after dress, oohing and awing or exclaiming in horror. The dresses are lace and sequined, form-fitting or A-line, each one shorter than the next. I remember, with a mix of pride and dismay, the dress I wore to my own eighth-grade dance, twenty years earlier. It had a floral print with puffy sleeves and a lace collar. At the time, I believed it to be the most gorgeous dress in the whole world. I paid $14.99 for it at T.J.Maxx with my own money. And I'm pretty sure it also had a matching headband… I remind myself to try to find a picture of it to show the girls. They will be appropriately horrified.

Laden with armloads of possible choices, Mikayla and Audrey, who has decided she will try on a few as well in solidarity, head for the dressing room. Geneva and I sit on a cream-colored bench and await the fashion show.

"You look good," she says. I give her a little smile.

"I feel better," I tell her. It's a pretty broad statement, but generally true.

"How are things with Daniel?" she asks, always one to get straight to the point. I give her a vague shrug, not wanting to think too much about the progress Daniel and I have made, fragile as it is.

Mikayla comes out of the dressing room in a short black dress with a cutout that leaves her lower back bare. She spins gloriously in front of the mirror, clearly in love with what she sees. She looks ages older than thirteen and beams with confidence. Geneva gives her a look that visibly deflates her, and she heads back to the fitting room for something more "age appropriate," as Genny puts it. Audrey comes out in a full-length gold sequin gown that she has pulled on over her t-shirt. The dress is so long it drags on the floor, and the sculpted bust hangs loosely around her chest. She uses both hands to hold it up, giggling uncontrollably. Mikayla appears again and doubles over in a fit of giggles at the sight of her sister. Geneva wipes tears of laughter from her face.

"I'm so glad they have each other," she whispers to me.

"When did they stop being babies?" I whisper back. She shrugs, shaking her head at her two girls, both just on the edge of growing up. A few misses later, Mikayla finally comes out in a white lace dress with a modest neckline that looks striking against her dark hair. It fits her slim body, but not too tightly, so Geneva approves.

"I love it," Genny exclaims, coming over to give Mikayla a squeeze. "Do you like it?"

Mikayla smiles, but then worry drops over her face.

"What is it, honey?" Genny asks.

"Um..." Mikayla starts, her face flushing bright red. "It's... it's... um... well, it's white... what if... *you know!*" She gives her mother a desperate look. It takes Geneva a minute to understand.

"Right, gotcha. Well, the dance is a few weeks away..." Geneva pulls up the calendar on her phone and they do some quick period math. "When was your last..." But Mikayla hushes her before she can say the word, and I cover my mouth with my hand to hide my smile. I get up and drift over to the nearest dress rack to give them some privacy.

My mind wanders back to memories of having to talk about uncomfortable things like periods and bras with my very old-fashioned mother and know-it-all sister. Mom had cautioned me back then that using tampons would mean I was no longer a virgin, information that was, of course, later debunked in the equally mortifying middle school "Reproductive Health" class.

I glance back at Geneva's girls, jealous of their bond and of the luxury of growing up in a time when facts about women's bodies are far easier to verify. But I also didn't envy those early days of womanhood when it felt like your cycle was always going to surprise you at the worst moment even though you religiously tracked it on a calendar. These days, I just keep a few loose tampons in my purse and don't even bother keeping track. In fact, I can't even remember the last time I...

I stop short, my hand poised over a rack of evening gowns, as my mind churns. The days, weeks, dear God, *had it been months? No, no, that can't be right...* I can't breathe in. The floor starts to tip toward me, and I grab the rack to keep my balance.

"Holy fuck," I say loudly, and out of the corner of my eye, I can see Geneva's head swivel toward me in alarm. I turn in her direction, and the girls are looking at me as well, shock clear on their faces. Several other women shopping nearby stop to see who is using such profanity in the Nordstrom dress department. I don't even see them.

"Ellie?" Geneva asks. Her image, with her two daughters, is copied over and over in the four-way mirror behind them. Mikayla is still wearing the white dress.

"I said holy fuck," I say, my voice sounding far away to my own ears. Geneva shutters at the word, glancing at the girls, but waits with a look of apprehension.

"What is it?" Her eyes wide as she takes a step towards me. I swallow and grip the dress rack with a very sweaty palm. I can't believe my immense stupidity. I can't believe something so obvious has happened, and I've completely missed it. I can't fathom what this will mean. I look at my sister.

"I'm pregnant."

I don't remember how I got through the rest of the night. But by the time I get to the police station the next day, my eyes are almost swollen shut. I cling to Daniel. He is holding me up.

The police grill me about Owen. Date of birth. Height. Weight. Eye color. Hair color. Birthmarks. Friends. Teachers. Family. Penchant for running off. I recite the answers over and over. I know every inch of him. I know how his hair smells after a bath. I know his favorite superhero. I know how much he hates to brush his teeth, but these things don't help.

They take Daniel to a separate room to ask him questions too. But he was at a client dinner last night. He wasn't there. Just me, and my only job was to take care of my baby, and I didn't do that. He's gone, he's gone.

They want to know the names of Owen's friends and who he might have trusted and where he may have suddenly decided to go that night. How ludicrous that my four-year-old would just choose to up and leave in his pajamas. I tell them this, angrily, slamming my fist on the desk, yelling for them to bring Daniel back, demanding they understand that someone has taken him, that they should, all of them, be out looking for him. They look at me with those half-pitying, half-patient faces. They've seen my kind before. They know the drill. They are processing me like paperwork. They tell me to wait.

CHAPTER 15

Getting pregnant with Owen had been, what I always thought of as, a line drawn in the metaphorical sand. A moment where I woke up and truly realized how a bit of carelessness could change a whole life. At my age, I should have understood all of that long before then, but live and learn, as they say. In the end I certainly didn't regret it—being Owen's mother is the most wonderful thing that has ever happened to me. But having been through it, I vowed to never be that careless again. Easy to say, of course. Fast forward seven years and pretty much every vow I've ever made about anything has been broken.

I've spent the last two years crippled by a series of overlapping emotions. Sorrow and guilt. Anger and frustration. Heartache and grief. Depression and desperation. And then, periods of complete nothingness. An abandonment of every human emotion, just to give the exhausted pieces of my mind a break. So when I finally put two and two together and realize that I am indeed pregnant, I should be able to sort through my catalog of emotions and pick the appropriate one, like finding the right folder in a massive filing cabinet of feelings. Instead, I switch to empty. Nothing. I don't want to tell anyone. I don't want to deal with it. I don't want to celebrate. I don't want to do anything.

The problem is that I've blurted it out to my sister and nieces, plus a few strangers at the mall, but I'm pretty sure they didn't care. While somewhat shocked, Geneva was cautiously excited, and the girls ecstatic. Geneva even had tears in her eyes when she hugged me and said it was wonderful news. The girls immediately started theorizing about the baby's gender. I tried not to throw up.

I begged them to give me some time to process things before I tell anyone. Geneva looked a little doubtful but agreed, thankfully, because I take two full weeks to tell Daniel. Two very long, tense weeks. We take some major steps backward in our progress during that time. Even Judith notes it, telling me I'm withdrawn and not participating. I feign exhaustion, telling them both I can't sleep, which is true. I lay awake at night, at times with my head on Daniel's shoulder, picturing how he will take the news. He's never actually said the words, *I don't want kids*, but I picture the way he used to stiffen when Owen tried to climb in his lap. Or his abhorrence of the cartoons Owen watched on the weekends. He wouldn't even sit in the same room. What will he do now with a child of his own?

I am so absorbed in worrying about Daniel's reaction that I don't let myself consider my own feelings. I keep them on neutral, nothing, telling myself that Daniel is the one to worry about. I consider that I might very well be doing this alone for the second time. Except this time, the father of my child would be walking out on us by choice, in case anyone was keeping score.

When I do finally work up the courage to tell him, I feel like I'm admitting to a crime. I sit down next to him on the couch and wait until he stops scrolling through his phone. He looks up at me.

"I'm pregnant," I say.

It's a jerk thing to do. No build up, no softening the blow, just blurt it out, maybe in some small way wanting to share the shock that I am feeling. I stare at his face, trying to read him as the information sinks in. Eyebrows raised. Eyes moving back and forth. A tiny smile that just barely flashes across his face, followed by a serious frown. He looks down at my stomach as if it might explode with children at any second.

"Oh," he says. He is quiet for a long time. "How?" It's a basic enough question, but I imagine he wants to know if I've done this on purpose.

"I wasn't thinking," I answer. The truth is that I stopped taking birth control almost a year ago. It wasn't a conscious decision. I ran out and never got around to getting more. Since we weren't having sex, there was no urgency. Add it to the list of things I had given up on, I guess.

"Are you ok?" he asks.

It's the right question, I suppose, the one that everyone has been asking me for a very long time. I'm not. I don't know what I am, but ok is most definitely not it. He moves closer to me and takes my hand, searching my face. He is asking what I feel in order to help him decide how he feels. I shrug, my eyes misting over. He puts an arm around me and pulls me to him. I let my head rest on his shoulder. We sit in silence.

"We'll figure it out," he says. But I'm not sure if he means the two of us, or the three of us.

On Tuesday, I tell Jane. Our sessions have been difficult lately, since I haven't felt ready to open up to her. When I finally do, she looks so relieved that I apologize. I feel like I've been lying to a friend.

"Congratulations. How do you feel?" she asks me.

"I don't know," I tell her.

"Were you planning on having more children?" she asks.

It's the one question I really don't want to answer. In truth, I'm having a hard time associating the fact with the outcome. I get that I'm pregnant. I just can't make myself see a baby at the end. I shrug.

"It can be a confusing time," Jane says. "I imagine that you are feeling a lot of different things." I nod slowly. I don't want to admit how little I've been feeling but she can read the tension in my face.

"Ok," she says. "Like I said, it can be difficult to process your feelings when you are dealing with something so monumental. But I know being a mother is something that's very important to you."

"I'm already a mother," I say. She smiles.

"Of course, you are. Being a mother to a new child doesn't diminish your relationship with your son. In fact, it just means that you will be even more ready to love and care for this child."

"But... I can't!" I say, wondering how she can be so naïve. "I CAN'T take care of a child. Look what happens!" Exasperated, I get up from the couch and walk across Jane's small office.

"Ellie..." she starts.

"No! You don't understand! ONE job. I had ONE JOB. And... and now I'm expected to, what? Try again? Like, I've got another shot? Like, oh well, messed up last time, maybe this time will go better?" I am almost shouting now. "That's INSANE! I shouldn't even be allowed to HAVE a baby! I'm... I'm..." But I can barely get the words out. I sit back down on the couch, my face in my hands.

"What was that last word?" Jane, who has been sitting patiently, watching me wave my arms and pace the room, asks gently. I lift my wet face.

"Unfit," I say, and the sobs take over.

Somehow, until this point, I've kept it to a few lone tears in Jane's office, but now I can't help it. I don't care if she thinks I'm crazy. I cry and cry, as she gently passes me a handful of tissues. I cry because I will fail again. Everyone already thinks I have. They will think I've just made a new kid to replace the one I lost, like it's a new cell phone or something. I cry because my parents will be so happy and they will dote on this child like they did Owen, but Owen will be forgotten and relegated to only memories. I cry because I don't know if Daniel wants this kid or not, if he will leave me and the baby, if I will be alone.

Jane lets me cry without comment. When the sobs have calmed to sniffles and hiccups, she reaches over and squeezes my hand.

"Ellie, you are not an unfit mother—I am certain of that. You can't use Owen's disappearance as the definition of who you are. You are a loving mother, that's completely accurate. You didn't abandon him. You didn't leave him. You didn't mistreat or abuse him. You loved him and cared for him and gave him everything he needed. What happened is not your fault."

I know she's wrong, but I don't have the energy to argue.

"I hate to say it this way, but lots of parents lose children," she continues. "Whether it be from disease or injury or accident or abduction or a million other reasons. Many of them have other children. You don't think it stops them from parenting their other kids, right? This is the same thing."

"But what if I lose this one?" I fight the urge to put my hand on my belly.

"You know the chances of that are very unlikely. But let me ask you a question. If you could go back in time and not have Owen, not have to live through the pain of losing him, would you do it?"

"Of course not," I say with complete conviction. She smiles a tiny smile.

"You will feel the same way about this child," she says. "Your love for this child will be just like what you feel for Owen. And no matter how long you get to have this child in your life, which will most likely be for a very long time, you will be glad to have him or her. I promise."

I want to argue. *How could I love anything as much as I love my son?*

"What if..." I start.

"What if you don't?" she asks. "You will. Don't let your fear control you, Ellie. Don't stop yourself from loving this child because you are afraid. This child deserves to be loved and cared for. And I know you will feel it. Let that love happen, and you will be fine. My guess is that it will even help you heal in the end."

I nod, but I don't believe her. As if a day could go by without feeling the pain that I always carry around with me. As if losing a child is ever something you can heal from.

CHAPTER 16

The following weekend Nathan throws a giant fortieth birthday party for Geneva. Daniel has agreed to go, even though I know he doesn't want to. He has been quiet and withdrawn all week. Neither of us have mentioned the pregnancy again. But I catch him watching me when I'm doing the dishes or reading on the couch. He looks like he's trying to figure me out. But he never says anything. Part of me wonders if he is silently planning his escape.

The last thing I'm in the mood for is a party, especially considering my doctor's appointment is on Monday. I had done an at-home test, silently praying for three long minutes in the bathroom, without really knowing what I was praying for, only to see the two blue lines I already knew were coming. But I've put off seeing the doctor, since I'm not ready to feign excitement quite yet. I also haven't told my parents. I figure I've got plenty of time for that, although maybe less than I think. It took three tries to find a dress in my closet for the party that didn't cling to my stomach.

We pull into Geneva's neighborhood and have to drive all the way down her street to find a place to park.

"No valets?" Daniel says sarcastically.

I give him a little smile, but he's not that far off. Nathan has hired caterers, and there are waiters walking around with little trays of hor d'oeuvres. The living room is decorated with huge stands of pink lilies in silver vases, and most of the furniture has been rearranged to accommodate the crowd. Geneva's and Nathan's friends, who are all dressed in absolutely gorgeous clothes that very clearly do not come from Target (where I got pretty much everything I'm wearing tonight), crowd every available space, many with champagne glasses already in hand.

My sister is the center of attention, much like at her charity events, this time clad in an ivory-colored dress with silver and white beading around the collar. Her hair is swept to one side in an old-Hollywood wave, and square-cut diamond earrings glitter at her ears. She is positively glowing. I marvel at how truly gorgeous she is, and wonder how on earth she can already be turning forty years old. Of course, I'm not that far behind her. Though anyone who saw us would guess that I'm the older sister.

I wave but don't want to interrupt whatever story she is telling to the enraptured group clustered around her. Daniel heads off to find a drink. I go upstairs in search of the girls. They are both in Audrey's room, dressed in sweet little pastel dresses that I'm certain their mother has picked for them. Audrey is lying on her bed; Mikayla is in the desk chair. They are both absorbed in their phones, as usual, ignoring each other. But I find it adorable that they choose to be together while they do it, avoiding the party in solidarity. They get up when I gently poke my head around the door after knocking. I get a hug from each of them, though they are notably more timid than usual. I grab them back before they slip out of reach and squeeze them tightly.

"I'm not gonna break," I whisper into Audrey's hair. She smiles at me, and I'm once again shocked that her head comes almost up to my chin now.

"How do you feel?" Mikayla asks.

"Oh, I'm fine," I tell her, waving the question away. "Why aren't you guys downstairs?" They glance at each other guiltily.

"We were just about to go," Audrey assures me. They both slip on ballet flats and we, begrudgingly on all our parts, head down to the party.

We wander around, the voices of the guests and the jazz music playing on the house's built-in sound system echoing through the high ceilings in every room. I nod hello to a few people here and there until we make our way to the kitchen. My mother is there, critically eyeing the trays of food, mentally adding up the calories to see if the enormous gourmet spread covering every available counter space will actually equal a hearty meal. The doubt on her face is so obvious that I have to smile and walk around the big white marble island to give her a hug. She kisses both of my cheeks.

"Hello, sweetheart. How are you?" she asks. I haven't seen her since the disastrous Sunday dinner almost two months earlier. "What have you been doing with yourself?"

"Keeping busy," I tell her. Which is true. I've been busy trying to hold my marriage together. Going to therapy. Avoiding the outside world for the most part. Daydreaming about how the hell I will survive the rest of my life. Incredibly busy.

She searches my face, and I wonder again what Geneva has told her.

"I've missed you, *cara mia*," she says, finally. "Your father has too."

"I know, Mom. I'm sorry," I say.

"What is wrong?" she asks, instinctively knowing that beneath my normal level of melancholy and darkness, something new is tearing me apart.

"Nothing, Mom, I'm good," I tell her, trying to brighten my face.

"You have a new job?" But I tell her no.

"I don't know what I want to do," I admit.

"What?" she says, confused. "Eleanora, you are good at SO many things." But she is my mother and has to say things like this.

At that moment, Geneva sweeps into the kitchen, looking all lit up inside.

"There you are!" she says to both me and the girls, who are sneaking chocolate-covered strawberries off of the dessert tray. "Dinner first!" she scolds them, but with a smile. "Have you said hello to the Bravermans or to Paul and Robyn?" she asks and sends them off to do their social rounds. She turns back to me.

"You look lovely. Doesn't she look lovely, Mom?" Geneva asks, tilting her head like I am a piece of art that she doesn't quite get, but is trying to appreciate. I shoot her a dirty look. She knows I haven't told my mother.

"She is always lovely," my mother says, always the first to criticize, but also to defend. She comes to my side and catches the look between Genny and I. "What?" she asks. "What is it?"

"Nothing, Mom," I kiss her cheek and scurry out of the kitchen before she can ask any more questions.

The rest of the evening drags on. I can't find Daniel, so I am forced to make small talk with Geneva's neighbors and co-workers. A few of them ask questions about the upcoming 5K race that Geneva is organizing for the foundation. Everyone assumes that I'm involved with the planning. They give me such strange looks when I say I have no idea. You would think I would have grown used to these awkward stares by now, but it continues to sting just a little every time it happens. I can feel my face burning under so much scrutiny. The room grows hotter and smaller despite the laughter, the lights, and the happy people.

I slip out the kitchen door onto the large back patio to get away for a moment. It's a chilly night for early June, and it hadn't occurred to me to bring a jacket. Daniel is there, a dozen steps away, tumbler of whisky in one hand, his phone pressed to his ear with the other. He is turned away, looking out over the sprawling lawn, which rolls back from the house in a wave down to a wooded area behind the large garden shed. Standing at the edge of the patio, lit only by the light coming from the living room windows, he remains half in the shadows. I can't see his face or hear exactly what he is saying. But I can hear the tone. And my heart sinks. He hangs up the phone, and when he turns, he is surprised to see me there. A shiver runs down my body.

"Who was that?" I'm not sure why I ask. I know who it was. I don't want to hear him say it.

"Just a work thing." He walks toward me, a little unsteadily. I can smell his breath from several feet away. "Don't worry about it."

"Daniel, please." I don't know what I am asking.

"What? I'm right here," he says, placing both hands on my arms. "Shoot, you are freezing, come here." He pulls me to him, and I let my head rest on his shoulder. It feels good for a second, but the knot in my stomach won't relax. Maybe I misheard him on the phone. "Should we go home?" he asks, and I nod.

We head back in to say our goodbyes. Geneva thanks us both and whispers an extra thank you in my ear when I hug her goodbye.

"We need to talk about the 5K, ok?" she says, always hopeful that I'll get more involved. I give her a faint nod, wondering what it will take to get out of it. I'm obviously not going to run, so maybe I can get away with a quick appearance.

We are standing in the front entry, just about to slip out the door. Daniel is shaking hands with my father, who has finally emerged from a long, serious conversation about irrigation systems with someone who is either a co-worker of Nathan's, or maybe their landscaper? I'm not quite sure. The girls are already drifting away back toward the stairs. I'm about to open the door when I feel a small flutter in my stomach, almost too quick to notice. I freeze and instinctively put a hand over the small bulge that has grown there. I wait for a moment, and then, there it is again. The tiniest kick. Suddenly, I can picture a minute foot and the smallest little toes. My heart beats so fast that I feel momentarily dizzy. I grab for Daniel's arm and pull him toward the door so we can leave.

At the last moment, I look back and see my mother standing in the doorway of the kitchen. She is watching me with a small frown. I realize my hand is still cupping my belly, and I quickly drop it and smooth out my dress. But she has seen me, and a curious look crosses her face. Her eyes brighten, and her mouth drops open. She steps forward, but I rush out of the door, and Daniel closes it behind him.

CHAPTER 17

I'm having a full-on panic attack in the waiting room of Dr. Woodlock's office. Sweat rolls down my back, and I lean forward, hoping that it hasn't left a wet spot on my shirt. The lights are too bright and I grab onto my knees, trying to make the room stop spinning. There are women all around me. Some with huge bellies swollen with late pregnancy, their faces mixtures of happiness and discomfort. Some have infants in carriers or strapped to their bodies. Those women have the specific look of messy, unkempt exhaustion that I remember so well. Others are teenage girls, their knees pressed tightly together as they anticipate with horror their first gynecological exam. I have been each one of those women. But I know none of them have been, or are anything like, me.

It's the same thing I feel in any room. Every face, every person has their own story. I know they each face their own hell at times, their own sorrow, their own shortcomings. But so few of them, probably none of them, no matter where I go, have felt what I feel every single day. None of them have had their child stolen in the night. Not one of these new mothers will put their child to sleep and find that they are not there in the morning. That is my burden, my hell to live in, day in and day out. It makes me hate them; it makes me envy them. It makes me, at times, completely unable to speak to them in a normal way. Because they don't know; they can't know.

The noise of the women and babies around me create a buzz that fills my head and I want to run away screaming. The smells are even worse. Milk and sweat and rubbing alcohol and whatever brand of cleaner doctors' offices tend to overuse. It fills my lungs, forbidding me from pulling in a whole breath. I can feel my knees trembling underneath my hands.

I sat in this room seven years ago with Owen inside of me, first little more than a foreign concept, but later an undeniable life force that filled me up and stretched my body. Toward the end, as he ran out of space, he would kick me in the ribs over and over until I felt like I must be black and blue on the inside. He would then, in turn, jab me in the bladder, making for some very frantic runs to the ladies' room. I had been here when I found out he was a boy. The ultrasound technician asked me if I wanted to know what I was having. I nodded, in awe that I was, so casually, about to find out this information that would determine so much of the rest of my life. Pink onesies or blue. Son or daughter. Little prince or tiny princess.

"Let me just finish my measurements," she had said. She clicked away at the machine, typing notes about the size of the baby's head and spine and heart. Finally, as I watched, in the little text box, she typed *OH BOY*. I looked up at her, and she was smiling down at me. "Congratulations!" she said. "A little boy."

A boy, I thought. *A boy. Crap. What the hell am I going to do with a boy?*

I had sat in the waiting room while Geneva gave birth to each of her daughters. She was so calm. So ready to be a mother. Once they had cleaned the babies up, we were allowed to go in and see them. My mother would stand guard over the bed, her face full of pride and happiness. Geneva would be sitting up in bed, her hair brushed softly around her shoulders, her face clean of makeup and still pink with effort. And there in her arms would be a wrapped bundle with a pink hat pulled low over a tiny face. A girl. Like us. I approached them in such awe, transfixed by the life that had just started. Mom and I would enclose them with our arms, a three-generation circle of womanhood, welcoming our newest member. And when it was Audrey's turn, it included a toddler, admiring her new little sister.

I understood girls. I bought my nieces little dresses and headbands and tiny shoes with bows on them. As they grew, it was Barbies and My Little Ponies and dress-up clothes. I would brush their hair and paint their nails and play pretend, continuing all the traditions of sisterhood. And while Genny and I had our competitions and pettiness, like all sisters do, I couldn't imagine growing up without her three steps ahead of me. So when the ultrasound technician said *boy*, my first instinct was fear. Would I know how to love a boy? Would I know how to play with him? How to relate to him as he grew? What would we do if not nail painting and princess dress-up?

My fears were all ridiculous, in the end. All it took was the moment they lay him, screaming and red-faced into my arms in that hospital room, and I was in love. He was my boy. My love. My son. Cradled against my chest, he stopped crying after a moment and opened his brand-new eyes and looked up at me. I know babies can't really see, and I know he didn't know me yet. But I knew him. I knew his kicks and his movements. I knew his heart and his soul. And I knew right then that we would have no trouble bonding at all.

I had brought Owen back to Dr. Woodlock's office for my six-week check-up. I dressed him up in one of the adorable little outfits my mother had bought for him. The nurses insisted he was the sweetest little thing, which he obviously was. He slept while Dr. Woodlock prodded my belly and asked about my milk supply and if I was getting any rest. I guess the black circles under my eyes were pretty telling. But I was in love, so none of it mattered. The dried spit-up on the shoulder of my t-shirt, the saggy postpartum stretch marks, the smell of baby wipes that seemed a part of me now — they were all part of taking care of this little man.

The door opens, a nurse steps out with a clipboard, and I squeeze my eyes shut, willing her not to say my name. I'm not sure if I can walk across this room full of women without falling down. I should have told my mother. I should have brought her with me. Or Daniel, but he is working and I'm still not sure how he's taking the news. Or Geneva, but she is far too happy about the baby. Even so, I'm such an idiot for always trying to do this stuff on my own. The nurse calls out someone else's name, and I let out the breath I didn't realize I had been holding.

I grip my hands together to try to keep them from shaking. I can't do this. I can't be here again. Waves of nausea crash over me, and I know I have to leave. I pick up my purse and get up, praying that my legs will hold me. I'm about the walk out the door when another nurse pops in and calls my name. I freeze. She has to say it again before I turn toward her. She smiles at me and beckons for me to follow her.

"Ok, hun, just hop up on this scale for me," she says. "Wait, you are gonna want to put your purse down." I fumble with it, and she helps place it on a nearby chair. "Are you alright?" she asks me. I nod and wipe my sleeve across my forehead, which is damp with sweat. "Ok, all set." She makes a note on her chart. After I give a very unsteady urine sample, she brings me to an exam room, where I strip down and arrange myself under one of those lovely paper sheets.

Eighteen minutes go by before the doctor knocks on the door and lets herself in. Eighteen minutes of deep breaths and pep-talking myself into staying. Despite that, I get up three different times, intending to get dressed and walk out, but I convince myself to sit back down every time. I don't want to talk to the doctor. I don't want to hear the words. I am not ready. I have to talk myself through every second until she finally comes in.

"Hi Eleanora, how are we today?" she asks, flipping open her laptop and scanning my record.

"Good," I say meekly.

"Looks like it's been a few years since we've seen you." She glances over at me, eyebrows raised.

It's true. It's been over two years. And suddenly I know what she is going to ask next. My chest seizes up, and I don't want her to say it. She is reading the chart, about to remember that I have a son. She will ask how he is. Her face suddenly collapses into a frown, and she moves closer to the screen, squinting her eyes. Then they fly open.

"Oh my," she says, mostly under her breath. Her lips draw together, and she turns to me, placing one hand over mine. "There's a note here about your son."

Thank God, I think, my eyes closing in relief. I don't know how they know about Owen, but I'm so grateful that I don't have to say the words myself. One tear slips out and falls, leaving a wet spot on my paper gown. She squeezes my hand.

"I'm so sorry," she says, and I nod. One more squeeze, and she moves back to the screen. "Ok, so you had a positive pregnancy test?" I nod, still not trusting my voice. "Well, your urine test here confirms it as well. Congratulations." Her voice is still tentative, trying to judge my reaction. I try my hardest to give her a little smile. She helps me lay back on the table and gently begins pressing on my stomach.

"Date of your last period?" she asks, her fingers roaming. I clear my throat.

"I'm not sure. I don't remember."

"Ok, no problem. We'll do a quick ultrasound to determine how far along you are."

"Oh, that's ok, I can tell you. I'm about eight weeks," I tell her. She raises her eyebrows again. "Well, I... um... well, my husband and I have only... you know... once in the last few months or... last year really..." I can feel my face burning. She nods.

"Ok, well, we'll do one anyway, just to make sure the baby is doing well." But I can hear the hint of a patronizing tone in her voice.

Fine, I think, *don't believe me*.

She has me dress and move to one of the ultrasound rooms. I'm calmer now, but being back in the room is like stepping back in time. I take a shaky breath and try to remind myself that they are probably used to crazy hormonal women. At least the room is dark. I try to quiet my racing heartbeat. The ultrasound technician comes in with a smile. She is young and pretty, with purple hospital scrubs and her hair tied back in a cute ponytail. She chatters at me about God-knows-what — I'm not listening — and busies herself with her machines before folding back my shirt and squirting a cold mound of gel onto my stomach.

"Ok then," she says. "Let's have a look." Only a few quiet seconds tick by before she says, "There we are!"

But my eyes are squeezed shut. I can't. Tears slip out from beneath my closed lids. I can't let myself see it, can't let myself love it. I can't allow my heart to give itself completely again. The technician looks away from the screen and sees my struggle.

"Oh, oh dear!" she says. She removes the ultrasound wand from my stomach and reaches for a box of tissues. "It can be a very emotional moment," she says, trying to assure me, assuming I'm just overwhelmed with joy at seeing my baby for the first time.

But she can't possibly understand. Can't comprehend how, if I see it, I will love it, just like I love Owen, with the same risk of being ripped apart by it someday.

After a few moments of sniffling and wiping at my eyes, I apologize to the nice young technician and tell her to do what she needs to do. She doesn't make small talk this time. Instead, she moves quickly through the motions, pressing here and there, running down her checklist. I stay turned away from the screen. All I can see is Owen's face. His four-year-old face, cheeks reddened by exertion on the playground. His one-year-old face, covered in blue birthday cake frosting. His newborn face, screwed up in anger when he was hungry or tired. After a few moments, she places a hand on my shoulder and asks if I want to see. I close my eyes again and shake my head.

"Ok, how about this? I'll print a few pictures and put them in an envelope for you to look at when you are ready. I'll write down the gender too, in case you want to know."

I don't look at her or thank her, even though she is being exceedingly kind. I can't move without wanting to curl up in a ball right there on the table and die. She gently wipes the gel from my stomach and smooths down my shirt and helps me to sit up.

"I'll just send the doctor in now," she says and quickly leaves.

I feel momentarily bad for her. She shouldn't have to deal with my mess. I wonder, not for the first time, why I even bother to leave my house anymore.

Dr. Woodlock slips into the room but doesn't turn on the light. The bluish glow from the blank screen is the only thing lighting the room. I can't bring myself to look at her. My eyes are swollen. I wipe my nose on the damp clump of tissues in my hand. Hardly the picture of thriving motherhood I'm sure she is used to. She sits on the stool and slides herself over to where I still sit on the table. She takes a deep breath, and I prepare myself for some kind of firm but gently pep talk about how, even though I've lost my little boy, I have to rally myself for this pregnancy, that my baby needs me and that I'm failing him or her already.

"Eleanora," she says, "I know this is hard." I keep looking down at my lap. "Kristin says you didn't want to see the baby?"

Here it comes, I think.

"I will," I mumble miserably. "I'm just not ready yet. It's still so early."

"Not that early." She looks down at the papers in her hand. "Looks like your timing is a little off."

What was she saying? She's not making any sense, and I feel a rising frustration. I just want to be out of this place. I straighten my shirt and start to stand up.

"Well, eight or nine weeks," I say. "Something like that, I didn't count it down to the exact day." I am annoyed that she is nit-picking. She puts a hand on my knee, urging me to sit back down. I finally look at her.

"You are further along than that, Ellie. According to the baby's size, I put you right around sixteen weeks or so." I shake my head.

"No, that's not right." I do get up this time. I need to get out of this dark room and get some air. I need to be alone to cry some more. I need my couch or my bed or my car at the very least. I need to be away from here, where everyone is looking at me, trying to figure out what's wrong with me.

"Ellie, please listen," she says, a little more insistently this time. "I know you are struggling right now. That's very understandable. But let's do whatever we can to make sure this baby is healthy. You are almost four months along, and you've had no prenatal care so far. Now, from what we can tell, the baby is healthy and doing well. But I want you to make sure you get your prenatal vitamins. Stop by the lab for your blood tests — we want to check your iron levels. Ok?"

"Four months?" I say slowly. I put my hand on my stomach, where there is an undeniable bulge. Was it that big before? Have

I been denying it to myself? But I know it's not possible. I can't make sense of it. I frown at the doctor. "Are you sure?" She nods.

With shaky hands, I collect my purse and the envelope and manage to thank the doctor before I leave. I am supposed to schedule my next appointment with the receptionist, but I walk straight out the front door into the warm June sunshine. It takes a concerted effort to put one foot in front of the other and get through the parking lot. I sit in my car but don't turn it on. I close my eyes to try to stop my head from swimming. I have eaten nothing today, and spots dance behind my closed eyes. The thought of my appointment had been so overwhelming this morning that I couldn't get any food down.

I open the calendar on my phone. *My math must be wrong*, I think. My mind is hurling thoughts around in my head. Nothing makes sense. I look back over the weeks. I went to the police station in early April. When I saw the picture of the boy who wasn't my son. That's the night when Daniel and I had…

But I couldn't remember any times before that. Not for months, maybe even a year. I know my memory is faulty, but I think I would remember this. I know there are periods of time I can't account for — hours or maybe even days I don't have a clear recollection of, but surely sleeping with my husband would have stuck in my brain when it had been such a sore point between us.

I flip further back in the calendar. Four months, she had said. What the hell was I doing four months ago? I see the appointment with Flavia on my calendar at the end of February. Something tugs at my memory, but I can't grasp it. The days after getting fired are a blur. I do remember Daniel being particularly frustrated and distant. It seems so unlikely that we would have slept together then…

Suddenly, my brain stops. *No*, I whisper out loud. But there, in the back of my mind, is a small flash of memory that makes no sense at all. Because if it's true, how can it be that I haven't remembered it until now? Again, my hand floats down to my belly and the small life growing there. Suddenly, I'm glad my stomach is empty. I grasp the steering wheel with both hands, trying to steady the shaking. But they won't stop, and my brain won't stop, and now I know, almost for sure, that I have, once and for all, ruined absolutely everything.

CHAPTER 18

Anton looks like he might throw up. I've appeared at the door of his apartment asking if we slept together. Who wouldn't be shocked? But he's not only shocked, he's hurt. Hurt that I don't remember, that my mind erased that night and what happened, pretending in fact that it never happened at all. My stomach twists and I think I might also be sick right here on the floor of his apartment. *What have I done?*

"So, you don't remember… anything?" he asks, a tiny wisp of hope in his voice.

But I shake my head, knowing that the conversation is only going to get harder.

"Not really… I'm so sorry, Anton. It… it happens to me sometimes. I blank out. I do things I don't remember. I don't know why. It's been happening since… since Owen's been gone. Not that it's any excuse."

I'm perched on the edge of the couch in his living room while he paces back and forth on the shiny hardwood floor. I've driven around all day, wasting time until I assumed he'd be home from work. It's rude of me to just show up, but I have to know what happened. And once I walk in, past Anton and his shocked-to-see-me face, and see his quiet, comfortable apartment, with pictures of his niece on the mantle, and his big, soft leather couch, and his work bag tossed on a kitchen chair, I'm certain I have been here before. Bits and pieces flash back, but I push them aside. I don't want to replay it in my head now. I don't want to remember. I only want the facts.

He finally sits down on the other end of the couch and leans over with his head resting in his hands. My stomach burns.

"I'm so sorry," I say again, and he looks up at me with a sad smile.

"I thought you were avoiding me because you were upset. I thought you regretted it, or that maybe you thought I had taken advantage of you because you were drunk. But I was drunk too!" he adds hurriedly.

"I would never think that about you," I reply, looking at him. His eyes are dark behind his glasses. "I assume it was, um, mutual." I have to look away again.

"Yes," he says so emphatically that I turn back. His expression makes me actually laugh out loud, and he smiles his big, wide smile at me. "Yes, it was." I can feel my face flush.

"Look," he says, sliding closer to me on the couch. He cautiously takes my hand. It feels odd. We are friends, and I've never thought of him like this before. My fingers are stiff beneath his hand. "I don't want to make you uncomfortable… but I think you are amazing and beautiful." I pull my hand back. Hurt flashes across his face. "Shit, I'm sorry. I'm just saying that I think you are great, and I don't want to lose you because we did something dumb one night. I'm hoping we can just forget it. I mean, you already have, right?" he says, trying to make a joke.

He has no idea.

"I'm married," I say, not meeting his gaze. "And yes. It was dumb." I get up from the couch. I can't stand his kindness. He doesn't even get how bad the situation is. But sitting here, faced with his sweet hopefulness, I can't tell him. He will be heartbroken. Or even worse, excited. I can't do it to him.

He stands up next to me, and puts one hand on my arm, turning me to him.

"I know that," he says firmly. "I'm not trying to mess anything up for you. I'm sorry for what happened. Please don't hate me. And please don't beat yourself up."

I nod, wishing he wouldn't stand so close.

"I'm sorry too." I pull my arm away and leave him standing there all alone.

What the flying fuck am I going to do now? is all I can think. I sit in my car in the parking lot of Anton's apartment building for a long time. For a while, I wonder if he will come after me. Maybe apologize and tell me he'll never bother me again. Or maybe profess his undying love for me and offer to take me far, far away from here. Instead, he doesn't appear, and I sit there alone wondering which one I would prefer to happen. I sit there until the summer night starts to fall. I can hear crickets chirping and kids playing on the playground in the falling dusk on the other side of the parking lot. For once, I don't scan their faces, looking for Owen. In fact, it doesn't even occur to me to look. They are someone else's children.

I finally force myself to go home, but the last person on earth I want to see is my husband. He will see right through me and know the horrible truth. That I've been unfaithful. That the child I am carrying does not belong to him. That our marriage is undoubtedly over. It's all real, and he will know it soon enough, but I don't have the strength to face it just yet.

When I do eventually work up the courage to walk through the door, Daniel is sitting at the kitchen table eating a sandwich and flipping through news stories on his phone. He looks up at me and narrows his eyes, no doubt seeing my puffy eyes and drawn face.

"What's up?" he asks. "Where have you been?"

"Sorry, I meant to text you," I say, avoiding looking at him as I toss my purse onto a kitchen chair. "I was out shopping with Geneva." But I realize my mistake a second too late. "I… um… left the bags in the car."

"Oh," he says, looking back down at his phone. He suddenly looks back up. "Hey, how did it go at the doctor?" My mind cartwheels.

"They had to reschedule. The doctor was sick. They moved my appointment to next week," I say, busying myself by wiping bread crumbs off the counter with a sponge.

"Hmm." He takes another bite of sandwich.

I put away the mayonnaise and cheese and load a few dirty dishes in the dishwasher. I'm sure he must be watching me, seeing the thoughts swirling around in my head, knowing that something is horribly wrong. I turn back around, but he is fixated on his phone. I let out a shaky breath.

"Well, I'm pretty tired," I say, not even having to try to let the exhaustion show in my voice.

"Uh huh," he says, not turning my way. I quickly walk out of the room, my knees shaking with every step.

Good God, what am I going to do?

What I actually do is leave. I pack a bag after Daniel leaves for work the next morning and text him to say that I've decided to visit my friend Anne. He asks if I'm ok, and I insist that I am. It sounds insincere even as I type it, but he doesn't question it, doesn't call to speak to me in person, doesn't ask me not to go. Instead, he says, "Have fun." Not "Have fun!" like he actually means it, but "Have fun" like he knows that it's the thing he is supposed to say.

I get in the car and drive away, inspired at the thought of endless hours alone in the car. Just before I get on the highway, I stop and buy a bottle of prenatal vitamins at CVS. The bottle is pink, and it has the outline of a woman with a protruding belly. Her outline hand curves around it, sheltering the imaginary outline baby inside. I stare down at her. She must be thrilled. I bet she's knitting little outline booties right now and dreaming up the perfect baby name. *The fucking drawing on the outside of the vitamin bottle is being a better mother than me right now*, I think. I throw the bottle in the back seat and drive away.

I leave town and head west. The weather is gorgeous, and the sun shines so brightly through the sunroof that I have to turn the AC on. Summer has arrived in New England and, like every year, we act like we've never known it before. People drive by in their open top Jeeps or with their windows rolled down, singing to the radio and feeling the wind blow through their hair. Everyone is already in tank tops and flip-flops, even though it's only in the low seventies. We endure so much winter here that summer is never taken for granted.

Past Springfield, the towns spread further and further apart. I'm often alone on the highway, speeding past the trees and valleys with the mountains in the distance pushing up against the sky. I alternate between racing thoughts and complete blankness. I prefer blank, so I work to stay there. When the thoughts become too loud, I turn up the radio and sing country songs loud enough to drown out the voices in my head. The longer I don't think about everything, the better I feel. I'm thrilled at the feeling of driving away, speeding off, leaving everything behind.

I pull off the highway at a rest stop just after Albany to get some gas and use the bathroom. I realize that I'm famished and end up ordering a sandwich and chips as well. Back in the car, I eat with one hand, relishing the feeling of the food sliding down my throat. I haven't been this hungry in a long time, and before I know it, the sandwich and chips are both gone. I lick the salt off of my fingertips and wish I had ordered more. I take a deep breath and feel the satisfaction of a full stomach. I feel a little nudge in my belly, and before I can let myself process the thought, I declare out loud that I've clearly eaten too much and should really watch my diet more carefully. I force any further thoughts out of my head.

The hours pass quickly, and before long, I'm winding through the farm country of upstate New York. The afternoon sun is shining down on the fields, and the whole world feels warmed up and content. I roll my windows down and let the country air flow through the car. It feels cathartic, sweeping away at least some of the constant tension and sorrow that surround me. *How many tears have I cried in this car alone?* I wonder. *Too many*, I think. *Far too many.* Even the thought of crying makes my eyes mist over, but I breathe in the clean air and shake my head, clearing those thoughts away. I'm sure there will be many, many more of them to come, but not today. Not right now.

It's almost five by the time I pull into Anne's driveway, and I feel a flash of sorrow that my sudden, solitary road trip is over. Anne's red Rav4 is parked in the driveway, and the front door of the house is open. She is expecting me. I had called early this morning asking if she would mind some company. She had said yes without hesitation, though I know she is incredibly busy. I'm sure she's left work early to ensure she would be home in time to welcome me. This should make me feel guilty that she's gone out of her way, but instead I feel a little glow of happiness. Someone actually wants me around.

I'm about to step out of the car when I freeze. Wants me around. Well yeah, sure she does, right now. She doesn't know the terrible thing I'm about to tell her. She doesn't know that I'm a cheater and an idiot and horrible mother. Suddenly, the lingering calm and quiet of the past six hours are shattered. *What will Anne say? What will she think of me?* I shouldn't have come. I lift my hand to restart the car and get the hell out when Anne appears on the front porch. She waves one hand in greeting and trots down the driveway towards me. I have no other choice than to get out and greet her.

The top of Anne's blonde head only comes up to my chin. She barely clears five feet and has such a youthful face that she still gets carded when ordering alcohol and has had to mountain climb her way up to become a junior partner at her law firm because she is constantly underestimated based solely on her looks. But Anne has more fight in her than men twice her size, and she takes incredible joy in besting the ones who doubt her. I have to stoop a bit to hug my friend, but it's worth it. She squeezes me close to her for a brief second, and I can smell the familiar coconut shampoo that instantly brings me back to our shared college dorm bathroom. Something tight in my chest loosens just a bit. She steps back and smiles up at me. Maybe, just maybe, she will forgive me, even if no one else will.

Anne's place sits on the bank of Lake Ontario. It's a small, 1920s two-story cabin Anne has been renovating one room at a time, doing a lot of the work herself. She has just recently finished the kitchen, she tells me, as I drop my bag by the stairs and follow her towards the back of the house. The kitchen is fresh and clean, all done in navy blue and grays, with a huge picture window and a sliding glass door on the back wall that show off the lake in all its glory. An open bottle of wine and two glasses already sit on the counter.

"It's fantastic to see you," she says, eyeing me. "How's everything?" Anne is not one to mince words or avoid uncomfortable topics.

I sit on a stool pulled up to the large blue marble island in the middle of the room. The counter is cold under my hands, and I have a momentary urge to rest my face on it. It would be solid and unyielding and might help keep the words I have to say from spilling out.

"Ellie?" she asks. I look up at her and just shake my head. I know my voice won't be steady if I try to say something. She comes around the island, closer to me. My eyes fill with tears.

"Oh, honey. You definitely need this," she says, pouring a very generous glass of wine and sliding it over to me.

I smile a little and bring the glass to my lips. The fruity smell fills my head, and I close my eyes in a tiny moment of bliss, before reality jerks me back. I put the glass down so suddenly that it clinks loudly against the counter. I am horrified by what I have almost done. Anne is frowning at me.

"What the…" She looks back and forth between me and the glass. Slowly, her eyes widen. "Wait, Ellie, are you…?" I put my head down on the cold blue counter and cry.

CHAPTER 19

I tell Anne everything. Or, as much of it as I remember, anyway. If she is shocked, she doesn't let it show. Instead, she brings me tea and covers me with a blanket and strokes my hair and brings me as many tissues as I need. She even gets me to smile when she says it's just like the mornings in college after we would go out drinking all night at the loud, grungy bars we would frequent.

"Good Lord, that feels like a lifetime ago," I say. We are laying on two lounge chairs on her back patio, watching the sunset cast long ribbons of orange and pink light across the water. My eyes are bloodshot and puffy and my voice has gone hoarse. I am exhausted but feel as though I've dropped the boulder that I've been trying to carry around unnoticed. We sit in silence for a while, watching bats swoop between the trees and listening to the frogs sing to each other. The peace is so absolute that I want to stay forever and never face the truth of what's happening in my life. After a while, Anne turns to me.

"Sweetie, I'm sorry to ask, but what will you do now?" I shake my head.

"I don't know," I say. "I have to tell Daniel, I guess."

"Well, yeah," she says. "You kind of do."

"He will leave me." I know this is true. I have no doubt in my mind. Cheating is one thing. Even if that were it and he found out, there would still be a chance we could fix things, considering what he has done. But this? Totally another level. I can't quite wrap my head around the fact that this is something I have done, that this is the person I am. Anne watches me struggle.

"El, you have to take a step back and look at the big picture. I honestly don't think it would have happened if you and Daniel were happy."

"Annie, I can't remember the last time I was happy. It's not Daniel's fault," I tell her.

"Maybe not entirely, but he certainly plays a part, don't you think?" she asks.

No, I think. *It's my fault. I do all of this to myself.* I shrug, knowing that she will disagree with me.

"Look, you know I love you and would never want to do anything to hurt you or make things worse, right? But I have to be honest." she says. I frown at her, not understanding.

"Ok," I say, still confused.

"Daniel is an asshole, and you will be better off without him." I look at her in shock.

"Why on earth would you say that?" I ask defensively, genuinely hurt.

"Well, the cheating is one thing," she says. "Not cool. But I've never liked him. He's too... smooth. Too calculating. I always felt like he only cared about himself."

"That's not true!" I say, sitting up and putting my tea mug down. "He's great; I've just been a horrible wife for the last two years. I'm the one that's failing, not him! What do you expect him to do when he has to deal with me all the time? How could anyone put up with it?" I am almost shouting at her.

"Ellie, you have completely lost sight of what is happening. You lost your child, for God's sake! You have had every right to mourn and be lost. Daniel should have been your rock from the start, and he hasn't been, not from what I can tell. Do you know what he said to me after Owen disappeared?"

"What?" I ask, crossing my arms, not sure I want to hear what she is about to say.

"You remember when I came to stay with you for a while?" I frown, trying to remember. The days and weeks after Owen's disappearance are so blurry. "About two months had gone by, there was no news on him, no real leads? Geneva called me, desperate because you would stay in bed for days, and then go out looking for him nonstop, wouldn't talk to anyone but the police, weren't taking care of yourself?"

My face floods with shame. I remember bits of it. Mostly the feeling, the cold fear in my stomach that has since settled into a constant ache that I've grown used to, day in and day out. But back then it was new and fresh and horrifically painful.

"So I came to stay with you for a while, to see if I could help," she continues. "Every day I sat with you, went out and searched with you, handed out fliers with his picture, did your laundry, made sure you were eating and showering."

I turn away, embarrassed that she has had to do this for me. But she grabs my arm.

"No, Ellie, I would have done anything to help you. I would still do anything to help find Owen, you know that. But Daniel? I dunno. He was barely there. He was so removed, so distant. I was there for almost three weeks and hardly saw him at all. And when I had to get back home to go back to work, devastated that I had to leave you at your lowest, do you know what he said to me?" I shake my head, not wanting to know.

"He said, '*How long do you think it will take for her to get over it?*'"

It takes a minute for me to react because the words she said don't make any sense. Get over it. Get over it. Get. Over. It. I hear it in my head over and over, but it isn't making sense. Get over it? Over my child? Over losing my son? No, he wouldn't. He couldn't possibly.

"No," I say, still shaking my head. "You must have heard him wrong." But my voice is low and hesitant, because I know Anne wouldn't have gotten this wrong. This thing that is so big and awful and painful.

"Ellie, I'm sorry. I wanted to give him the benefit of the doubt, so I didn't tell you. But now, considering everything?" Her voice trails off.

My mind is still spinning. My eyes burn, but I don't have any more tears at the moment. What do I do with this information? He was mourning too. He was confused and upset, I tell myself. It can't be right. *Deny, deny, deny.* I try to force the door closed on the thoughts swirling around in my head and the squeezing feeling in my chest. I can't look at Anne. I'm not mad at her. But she's known this all along, this horrible thing that Daniel has said. What am I supposed to do now? I gather up the blanket and the tissues and the cold tea. My words catch in my throat, threatening to choke me.

"I'd like to go to sleep now," I whisper, looking down at the stone patio floor, wishing it would open beneath my feet and pull me down into the darkness.

I wake up the next morning in the big bed in the guest room of Anne's house, the sun filtering in through the curtains, leaving warm patches on the soft yellow duvet. I stare at the dust motes dancing in the beams of light, softly swirling as they drift up and down on invisible drafts of air. I can hear birds singing in the trees and the sound of the lake gently lapping against the shore outside of the open window. The smell of eggs and bacon drifts up from the kitchen, and I can hear Anne moving around downstairs.

My eyes are scratchy and swollen, my throat dry, and my bladder achingly full. But none of it is motivation for me to get up and break the stillness of the room. My heart and my head ache. *Just when I think things in my life can't get any worse, here we are.* I laugh in my head at my own melodrama. I sound like every depressed person ever. I'm nothing original or special, unless you count the extraordinary ways in which I've messed up. I feel destined to be sad, entrenched in my own misery, and I can't see a way out. I dread every morning. Even this morning, beautiful and peaceful as it seems, safe and welcome as I am at Anne's house, even this one is no better than every day that I wake up now. And just like every morning, I can't fathom how I will possibly get through the day.

Anne's gentle knock at the door finally gets me to move. She greets me with a hug and an apology for what happened last night.

"I'm sorry I upset you — that wasn't my intention," she says, over plates of breakfast in her kitchen. "I just want you to know that you will be ok… with or without him."

I give her half a smile, because I know she means well. I just don't know how to process what she's told me. I believe her, if I'm being honest with myself. I love my husband, but I know he's not perfect. He has always been a bit reserved, always holding back somehow. We aren't a 'tell each other everything' kind of couple. We never had those stay-up-all-night-talking kind of moments. But I had always told myself that it kept the 'magic' alive somehow. I mean, other couples pee with the door open. I can't even imagine.

Early on, there was romance. Dates and wine and hand-holding and sex. But we always had a sensible overtone to our relationship, a kind of satisfactory arrangement for the both of us, rather than a heart-pounding, blood-rushing need to be together. And it worked well enough for a while. Until we lost Owen, anyway.

I told myself that Daniel just wasn't a sentimental, passionate kind of person. But I had seen his face in the restaurant with that woman. I had felt their intimacy from the other side of the room. Even in that short moment, it was obvious that he had with her something he never had, and never asked for, with me. I hadn't given it to him, or else I just wasn't the person he wanted it from.

I confess these terrible feelings to Anne, who insists that they aren't terrible feelings at all.

"Look, I'm not one to judge other people's relationships, El, but yours doesn't seem to be working on any level. Regardless of the... I mean, of your pregnancy, he doesn't seem like the kind of guy you should be putting any effort into."

"I'll be alone, Annie," I say. "Actually, wholly, completely alone. I don't know how I'm going to handle it."

"Bullshit," she says, in her no-nonsense way. "You have me; you have your sister and parents and your nieces."

"Yeah, and you all have your own lives to worry about," I answer.

"You are part of it, Ellie. I promise you that not a single one of us resents having you in our lives."

I have my doubts but don't voice them. I know I am a burden to everyone, not that they would ever admit it.

"What about the father?" she asks. "Clearly there is at least a little something there."

Anton. A wave of guilt passes through me. I should have told him. Instead, I practically yelled at him and walked out. *How will I tell him?* I just shake my head. It has to happen. I just have to figure out what the hell to do first. My eyes fill with tears at the thought. Anne puts her hand over mine.

"Hey," she says. "You've got time. You'll figure it out. And I'll be here to help," which is enough to make the tears spill over and land on my plate of cold eggs.

"In the meantime," she says, popping up from her chair and whisking the plates away, "I think you could use some distraction. Get your ass in the shower — we've got places to go."

We spend the day shopping, walking around the farmer's market, driving past the vineyards and lakes that surround her small town. We stop for lunch, and later for coffee. We talk about everything except me and my problems. I realize how out of touch with current events I have let myself become. I used to watch the news religiously, sure that I would catch sight of Owen or get news of him from the TV, even while knowing it wouldn't happen like that. Even knowing it would be a phone call from Detective Luzcak if he had been found didn't stop me back then. It felt like one of the few proactive things I could do to help find him, even though I knew in my heart that it was useless.

Lately, I have been too wrapped up in my own sorrow to look to the outside world. World leaders have changed, disasters and terrorists have struck, discoveries have been made, fame for some has come and gone, and I have mostly missed it. It makes me feel yet another wave of guilt. *What kind of mother am I, not knowing the world I have brought my child into?* The thought stops me. *Children. Not my child. My children. Holy shit.* I look down and smooth my shirt to see if I look pregnant.

"You ok?" Anne asks, watching me. We are driving back to her house, the backseat full of fresh ingredients that Anne has promised to turn into a delicious dinner.

I nod, lost in thought.

We have a relaxed evening, Anne cooking while I sample the food and pretend to help. She doesn't even let me do the dishes. The sunset beckons us out to the porch again, its beauty and peace undeniable.

"No wonder you love it here," I tell her, and she smiles.

"I know it's not the most exciting corner of the world, but I wouldn't leave it for anything."

There is a serenity in her face that I envy. It occurs to me, quite late I admit, that she is the kind of alone that I am afraid to be. No children, unmarried, strongly self-sufficient and independent. Anne has told me before that her work is her life. Her relationships with her friends are incredibly important to her, but she is happy to go home to her own space at the end of the day. She dates on occasion but, she has admitted to me in the past, few men are comfortable with a woman so confident in herself and determined to be exactly who she is.

Her tranquility is infectious, and I snuggle down into the cozy woolen blanket I've wrapped myself in and let my mind remain happily blank, focusing not on the chaos of my life but on the brilliance of the stars over the lake, the sound of the breeze in the pines, and the brief, but very welcome, moment of peace.

CHAPTER 20

When I wake the next morning, I find Anne furiously typing on her laptop at the small desk tucked into the corner of her living room.

"Sorry," she says, not looking up, "just a few emails I have to answer. I'll get some breakfast going in a minute."

But she is squinting at the screen, a grimace on her face, and I know I've kept her away long enough. A few minutes later, I deliver her a freshly toasted bagel with cream cheese and a big mug of coffee. She looks up in surprise, and I feel good that I can help out in even this small way. I slip upstairs to shower and pack my things.

"I'll let you get back to it," I tell her, and while she politely protests, I can see the tiny bit of relief in her eyes. I sprung this visit on her at the last minute, and she had dropped everything to wait on me hand-and-foot. I wrap her in a huge hug and thank her.

"I don't know what I'd do without you," I tell her. And we both promise not to let so much time go by between visits again. Which is what we always say. She squeezes my hand one last time through the car window and waves from the driveway as I drive away.

Several hundred miles of sunlit road stretch between here and home. I feel calmer than when I faced them from the other end, but I still haven't figured anything out. Before I pull on to the highway, I pause for a school bus that is stopped to let students board. I can hear the kids' voices through my open window. It's a beautiful, sunny morning toward the end of the school year, and they can hardly contain their excitement. They bounce from seat to seat, leaning over to giggle with their friends or hand notes or books or other small things back and forth. There is a joy radiating from the big yellow bus, and I don't envy their teachers the task of keeping them quietly at their desks for the next six hours. *Owen never got the chance to ride a bus*, my brain reports, and my stomach begins to clench with its usual pain.

But a memory, both painful and sweet, pushes the thought out of the way. When Owen entered the preschool program at his daycare after turning four, moving from the "playroom," where it was a toddler free-for-all the whole day, to the more structured "classroom," where his name was taped to a desk and he began the joys of formal learning, picking out a backpack was quite possibly the hardest decision he had ever made.

The Back-to-School section at Target is a land of joy and sorrow, brimming with the excitement of a brand-new box of crayons (oh sweet glory!) but tinged with the sadness (on the kids' part anyway) of another summer almost having passed them by. The feet-dragging, whining, and complaining was not always just on the part of the children, either. They should have been selling bottles of wine in the same aisle, but the stores hadn't put that idea together… yet.

Owen showed no reluctance. No feet-dragging. He hopped down the aisle, both feet together kangaroo-style, until he stood in front of row-upon-row of brand-new backpacks. Star Wars, Batman, Lego, Pokémon, Avengers… the choices went on and on. His eyes bulging, his little dark head turning back and forth, as he tried to process the possibilities.

"Ok, buddy, what do you think?" I asked him, scrolling through my phone with one hand. I still had several calls to answer that evening and groceries to buy, so I was hoping our Target trip would be a brief one. His small fingers reached out to touch first this backpack, and then another one. The Hulk, maybe? Or dragons and castles?

"Do you see any you like? What about this?" I asked, holding up a Superman one that had a detachable cape. But he didn't answer. He walked slowly down the aisle, his little Stride Rites not making any sound.

I put Superman back on the rack, sighing at his slowness. We really needed to make this fast. Maybe we should have waited for the weekend when Daniel wouldn't be on his way home from work, anticipating dinner and a quiet evening. I opened my mouth to tell Owen to hurry, to make up his mind, but his stillness stopped me. My son was so rarely motionless and calm. His normal energy level was go-go-go, as he had been moments before walking through the parking lot and down the aisles. He had chattered endlessly on the way to the store, filled with thoughts and ideas about what he was going to pick out and how fun preschool was going to be.

He had shown some anxiety when I first told him he would be moving up to the preschool room. He would be leaving the teachers he had been with almost since birth and some of his smaller friends who weren't old enough to graduate with him. He knew every toy in that room, had a pile of his favorite books, and knew just where his coat and "nap buddy" (aka favorite stuffed animal du jour) belonged in his cubby. A whole new room sounded like too much change for him to deal with. But a brief visit, while holding tightly to Mommy's hand of course, including a tour of the shelves of BRAND-NEW books for him to choose from, seeing his name written in bold capital letters on the desk, and a quick overview of the preschool toys (especially the massive box of Legos), and he was sold.

The next weeks were filled with his imagination-sparked musings on the mystery and wonder that was sure to take place in the preschool room. The stories often involved Peyton, Owen's "bestest friend" from the toddler room, who would be one of the children moving up at the same time.

"Peyton's mom got him a Lego Batman backpack!" Owen had told me from his car seat on the way to Target.

"Lego and Batman? Two birds with one stone. Nice call, Stephanie," I said, admiring the work of Peyton's mom. Owen wasn't listening.

"I have to get something even better!" he piped from the back seat.

"We'll do our best!" I had promised him.

So, standing there in the aisle, seeing his complete speechlessness, I made myself stop. Put my phone away. Shifted my heavy purse so I could squat down next to him. He turned to me, his eyes huge and round.

"Don't worry," I told him. "We'll find it." His sweet smile in return was everything.

And on the first day of preschool, my kiddo bounced into school with the coolest Minecraft backpack you have ever seen, with a Spiderman key-chain attached to the zipper for good measure.

I picture his still-plump little legs as he walked up the steps to the school, me trailing a few feet behind him, his back-to-school haircut framing his changing face. And even though we had walked into the building hundreds of times, it hit me hard that he was growing up so damn fast and there was nothing I could do but hold on for the ride. The memory, bittersweet as it was, makes me smile, and for once, the happiness of the memory overrides the pain, and my stomach settles back to its normal anxiety level. That is, until the driver in the car behind me lays on their horn, jerking me back to the moment. The bus and the kids are long gone, and I am holding up traffic, lost in thought.

I lurch the car forward and pull onto the highway, shaking my head to clear my thoughts. How easy to swing back to those happy days, stressful as they were at the time. Between work and motherhood and marriage, my life was so full. Most days, I didn't stop moving from the time I woke up until I fell, exhausted, into bed at night. Now the days often seem endless. Pointless. I know I need to figure out what the hell to do with the rest of my life. With or without my son. My heart tightens at the thought. But then, for a brief second, I picture a tiny body in my arms, helpless and innocent. A small weight snuggled against my chest, our breathing in sync as they fall asleep, tiny mouth gaped open. Just as quickly, the image flashes away, a heavy curtain drawn tightly around the feeling. I take a deep breath and refocus on the mess I'm headed toward with Daniel.

The hours on the road fly by. I practice what to say, my voice shaking as I try rearranging the words, but they never come out in a way that will lead to things being ok. The truth is too ugly. I can't figure out how to make myself hurt him in this way. I think of the woman in the bar, the weeks he disappeared, the words he said to Anne. But they all feel inconsequential when compared to what I have done.

By the time I pull up to the house, I'm sweating behind my knees and under the thick mat of hair clinging to my neck. I see with a sick feeling in my stomach that Daniel's car is in the driveway, even though it's only just past four o'clock. I realize I haven't heard from him since I left. A tiny spark of fear flashes through me. I check my reflection in the rearview mirror, smoothing down my hair and rubbing some color into my cheeks. *Why am I bothering?* I wonder. But I know why. I'll walk in that door, and after I open my mouth, he will never, ever see me as the same person again. I swallow as that thought really sinks in. I wonder, for the millionth time, why the hell I'm even here.

I let out a shaky breath and turn off the car. *Only one way to go from here*, I tell myself. I turn to grab my bag from the back seat, and I see the bottle of pink vitamins laying on its side. I grab them, trying not to look at the outline mom on the label, and shove them into my purse. *Time for that later*, I think.

As I walk to the door, I brace myself for the same coolness and indifference that Daniel has shown me since I told him I was pregnant. I straighten my back, trying to make myself ready for what I'm about to do. I try to force calmness into my face and body so that I don't look like a crazy person. But as I walk in, I almost trip over a suitcase and Daniel's gym bag, which are lying right inside the front door. For a moment, I am annoyed that he would be so careless and go to push the things out of the way when I see him standing across the living room in the doorway of the kitchen. His face is still, but angry. I've never quite seen this look on him before, at least not directed at me. But he is looking at me now.

"What's going on?" I ask him, stepping over the bags. He just looks at me. "Are you going somewhere?" I'm afraid to walk toward him.

"Yeah," he says, finally. "I'm leaving. I was hoping to be gone before you got back." My heart pounds in my chest.

"What do you mean?"

"Well, there are a lot of things I can take. Your depression, your anxiety, your unemployment, you checking out of our marriage." His voice is crisp, each word is clipped like he can't get them out quickly enough. "But I never would have expected this from you." He turns and walks into the kitchen. I follow behind him to see that he is picking things up off the kitchen table and shoving them into his work bag—a phone charger, some headphones, a pile of bills.

"Daniel, please. What happened?" He doesn't respond. "Please, Daniel. Say something." He turns to me, a look of disgust contorting his face.

"There's a lot of things I'd like to say to you," he says, his voice starting to rise. "I've tried my hardest to make this work. And you just shit all over it. I'm done." He slings his bag over his shoulder and shoves past me toward the front door.

"Wait, I don't understand," I plead, trying to hold it together. This is what I've been preparing for, but I haven't said the words yet. He's two steps ahead. I can't figure it out. He spins back around to face me.

"I saw the ultrasound, Ellie," he says, spitting the words at me. "I'm not an idiot."

The words slice through me, and I put one hand on the door frame to steady myself. So he knows.

"It's not my baby, is it." It's not a question.

My mouth hangs open. I can't think of what words to say. My eyes fill with tears. I want to tell him I had made a mistake. That I don't even remember it. That I thought the baby was his up until a few days ago, that I wasn't lying to him on purpose. But nothing comes out. I look at him, knowing this is the end. He takes my silence as acknowledgement. He slowly nods and I watch the green of his eyes, the eyes that once looked at me with love and kindness, with empathy and understanding, darken and turn away.

"I'm so sorry," I manage to whisper. He makes a disgusted noise in the back of his throat. The door slams shut behind him, and he is gone. Just like that.

The ultrasound is on the kitchen table. An estimated length of gestation in weeks is printed in small white letters in the top left corner along with my name and the date. Everything he needed to know. I sink onto the kitchen chair, the small bulge of my stomach now feeling like an iron weight, pushing against my skin. I pick up the ultrasound picture, which Daniel has pulled from the envelope, but I don't look at it. Instead, I think about Daniel. His gentle hands, his handsome smile. I think of our first date and all the flirting and teasing. The happy dizziness of falling love. His sweet words when he proposed and the cool metal of my engagement ring when he first slipped it onto my finger. Those days seem so far away, and now they are gone. The hollowness inside of me gapes wide open, echoing and empty. It's a feeling I'm used to. A deep knowledge of my own, self-inflicted failures. But I don't cry. I'm too exhausted. Too broken.

I put the ultrasound facedown on the table so that I don't have to look at the gray, wavy image. And there on the back, one small, handwritten word. Four tiny letters. G-I-R-L.

He's missed breakfast, now lunch, now dinner. He's hungry, and I can't feed him. He's in pajamas, and I can't dress him. He'll have needed the bathroom, and I wasn't there to help him. He must be terrified, wherever he is, and I can't comfort him.

I can't sit still. I can't breathe. Dear God, where could he be? The police tell me to wait. I want to look for him, but we've already been all over the neighborhood and to his school and to the playground and his friends' houses. He's not in any of those places. Not in the woods behind our house. Not in the fields next to the supermarket down the street. But he is somewhere, and it's almost his bedtime again, and I can't put him in his bed like I did last night. They have to find him; they have to bring him home. Because he should be here. This is his home. I am his mother. But he's not here, and I can't hold him and make it all better.

My parents are here at my house. My mother prays. My father paces with me, steadying me. They wait with us. Wait for a call, a sign, a signal that he's been found. We wait for the policemen in the patrol car parked in our driveway to come back inside and tell us the good news. Because it has to be good news. Dear God, don't let it be bad. Let him be found. Let him come home.

CHAPTER 21

I stare at Jane's shoes. She's wearing blue platform penny loafers, with actual pennies tucked inside. They are shiny with a four-inch heel, and she has paired them with white ankle socks, neatly turned down into cuffs. For once, she does match, her shoes complimenting the splashy blue and pink flowers on her billowy skirt. I try to picture her walking into a store, seeing the shoes and thinking *Yes, you are coming home with me!* But it seems impossible, because who on earth would pick those shoes and then, even worse, throw them on with ankle socks?

For a brief second, a flash of worry cuts through me. I'm trusting someone to try to help me navigate my shit-show of a life, and she dresses like a five-year-old. Or, at the very least, a seriously stylistically impaired person. *Maybe she's as crazy as I am*, I wonder. And talking to her is just making me crazier. The blind leading the blind. Except it's worse because she's tricked me into believing that she's helping me. And I'm even paying her to do it. *What am I doing here?*

While I stare, unblinking at her shoes, Jane is taking several slow breaths, trying, I imagine, to process the fact that I've just told her I'm not carrying my husband's baby. That it is, in fact, the result of a one-night stand with a former co-worker that I have almost no memory of. She had let the shock flash across her face for a brief second before she calmed her features and started some kind of breathing exercise. Thus leaving me with plenty of time to analyze her fashion choices. Eventually, she clears her throat, and I look up, hoping she can't read my mind and know that I'm so shallow as to judge her by her shoes.

"How did Daniel take the news?" she finally asks.

"Oh, he left me. So that's done. Put another check in the *Failed* column, am I right?" I say, giggling. I know I sound crazy. But I think I just might be, so it's cool. Jane doesn't respond to my attempted joke.

"Have you told the father?" Her voice is calm.

"Nope. Doesn't sound like something I really want to do right now. I mean, what would I say? Sorry, Anton, I've got your baby in here. No clue how to handle this, but she would probably be better off with just about ANYONE else as a mother, so you're kinda screwed on that account," I say.

"She?" Jane asks. That wipes the lunatic smile off my face. I look down at my lap.

"Yeah. It's a girl," I say. I've had a few days to process this. Again, I can't quite align the words "it's a girl" with the idea that I will soon be raising a daughter. Pictures of tiny pigtails and frilly dresses and pink onesies and dolls and pajamas with little hearts and kittens on them keep flashing through my mind. They are memories of Mikayla and Audrey, but now they have a stranger's face. A child I don't recognize. Surely not mine.

"Have you given any thought to what you are going to do?" she asks.

As if I've just been sitting around NOT thinking? Of course I've given it thought. It's all I do. But there is no answer. No options. No path where good things happen. I'm an about-to-be divorced, single, pregnant lady with a lost kid. What the hell could I possibly do next? I glance up at Jane as she waits for my response. These are the types of rants I normally keep to myself. I don't want her to think I'm an asshole or that I don't appreciate her help. So I just shrug.

"C'mon, Ellie," she prods. "This is serious stuff. I know you've been thinking about it. Tell me." She's pushing more than normal.

"It doesn't matter how much thought I give it. I'm screwed. No matter what," I tell her.

"Well, I'm not saying this is the ideal situation, but I don't think all hope is lost," she says, as if I've had hope in God-knows-how-long. "Given everything you've told me, and with the knowledge that you had been actively working to make things better, do you feel you were in a happy marriage? Was it a marriage that was going to be fulfilling and satisfying to you in the long term?"

I don't answer her. She's right, of course. Just like Anne had been, even though I didn't want to admit it at the time, nor am I ready to admit it now. Daniel and I were not happy. Not lately anyway. But he was one of my only life rafts. The ones I have left are becoming fewer and fewer and keep drifting further apart. I picture myself in the middle of a stormy ocean, with the edges of boats slipping off into the fog and out of reach. I can feel the water closing in over my head, nothing below me but sweet, dark, cold oblivion.

"What does it matter?" I ask. "Happy or not, at least I had someone. Now I'll be alone."

"Will you?" She looks pointedly at my belly. I frown.

"Alone with a baby, even better," I mumble. Jane takes a deep breath.

"I'm not saying it will be easy. But you've got the support of your family. And perhaps the father. That's something you will have to figure out. And the sooner you do it, the better."

After I leave Jane's office, I do truly consider going to Anton's. But it's eleven o'clock on a Tuesday morning, and I know he won't be home, which is the excuse I make for putting it off. Clearly a text or phone call won't cut it. I sit in my car, totally at a loss for what to do next. I don't want to go home. I've been sitting there alone for the last four days, avoiding all human contact and burying myself under blankets and bad TV, haunted and surrounded by both Daniel's and Owen's things.

I'm at such a loss I would even consider going to see my sister, but she and Nathan and the girls left yesterday for their two-week trip to Italy. She had texted me a few times over the weekend to see how I was doing. While she didn't mention the baby directly, I know she is dying to talk about it and to make sure that I'm taking care of the both of us. But I haven't answered her, not knowing how to break the news about Anton being the father and Daniel leaving me. I sigh, glad that I have some time before I have to confess all of that information.

I'm certain Geneva still hasn't told my parents. If she had, my mother would have appeared at my door, knitting needles in hand with a halfway completed baby blanket already in progress, along with a hearty helping of guilt for not telling her sooner, both delivered in her infuriatingly contradictory way. I breathe an even deeper sigh, knowing where I need to go. Jane and Anne went out of their way to point out that I'm not going to be alone. But neither of them can understand just how disappointed my mother will be in me once she knows the whole story.

Of the many things I've failed at, being a good daughter is near the top of the list. My mother has called countless times since Genny's party, but I haven't answered or returned her calls. I can only imagine what she will think of these new events. She could never hide how ashamed she was of me for getting pregnant with Owen. That a daughter of hers would be so careless, so immoral, was unthinkable to her. But I was too busy being hurt by her reaction to consider her feelings at the time. Now I've done something a million times worse. Every instinct tells me to run in the other direction, but I can't hide from her forever. I pull up to my parents' house before I've had time to think it all the way through.

The late morning sun is shining through the sliding glass door in my parents' kitchen, lighting up the room in a warm yellow glow. My mother is folding laundry at the table when I walk in, sorting towels and sheets into precise, color-coordinated piles. The towels are frayed at the edges and the sheets are probably twenty years old and they have all faded from their original bright greens and pinks. But Mom folds them as if an army drill sergeant will be coming around to inspect her work. She lets out a little exclamation of happiness when she sees me and drops the pillowcase she is folding back into the basket to come hug me, bringing the warm scent of dryer sheets along with her. It's unlike me to drop by unannounced, and I feel a momentary flash of happiness at her joy in seeing me there.

"Where's Dad?" I ask, as she walks back to the table.

"At the office," she tells me, rolling her eyes.

My father semi-retired a few years ago but has a hard time sitting still. He therefore still oversees the occasional project at the contracting company he ran for over thirty years, much to my mother's annoyance.

"Just for a meeting," she tells me. "He will be home for lunch. You can eat with us." She leaves no room for argument.

"Thanks, Mom," I say.

But food is the last thing on my mind. I watch her fold the last of the linens and place them neatly back in the basket so she can transport them to the carefully organized and cataloged linen closet later on. She places the basket on the floor and gets me a glass of water without asking if I'd like one and gestures for us to sit at the kitchen table. I trace my finger along the worn edge of the wood, wondering how many tough conversations I've had while sitting right in this spot. About school and grades, about boys and dating, about responsibility and chores.

Somehow, we always found something to disagree about while I was growing up.

Today will be no different, I know. My mother watches me in silence, her head slightly cocked to the side. I meet her eye and know instinctively that everything I am about to tell her won't be a total surprise. Somehow, she always knows me better than I expect she will.

"Mom," I start and die inside at the hope in her eyes. But leading with the news about the baby was not the way I intended to do this. "Mom, I'm sorry." She frowns.

"Sorry for what?" she asks.

"There are some things I need to tell you, and they won't be easy to hear."

"Ok," she says.

"Daniel and I have decided to separate." Her eyes widen and the creases around her mouth deepen. She is unprepared for this. Her mouth drops open to speak.

"Wait," I tell her. "It's for the best." She starts to shake her head.

"But... but... are you?" She looks down at my stomach. I take a deep breath and nod.

"Yeah. I'm pregnant." I have to look away from her.

"Then, what are you talking about? You make it work! God has given you a child, and you have to do the right thing. A child needs their mother and father." I flinch at the words. They are so terribly hurtful, though I know it's not how she means them.

"You do not run away from a problem, Eleanora," she says, the anger rising in her voice. "This is crazy talk. Everybody has problems, but you work on them. And now you have been blessed, and you want to throw that away? No. No, child."

Child, she calls me. It would almost be funny if it wasn't so awful. I wish to God that Geneva was here. She is much better at calming our mother down than I am.

"Mom, please," I start.

"NO, Eleanora. I am serious," she says, rising from her seat, the legs of the chair scraping across the worn linoleum floor. "You cannot do this. You are making a mistake. Think of your child." She leans across the table, pointing a finger at me.

"Mom, listen," I try again.

"NO, you listen. FOR ONCE!" she yells, her face flushed and angry. "Listen to me. Stop being so selfish! You think marriage is supposed to be perfect? You think everything is supposed to be easy and wonderful but that is not real life. What is so bad that you can't make it work, huh? Sometimes you have to put some effort into things instead of running away. What do you think is out there that is so much better? You think you will just find another husband to raise a child with? Just like that? You are kidding yourself. You are asking too much."

"MOM, you don't know what you are talking about!" I yell back at her. "I'm doing the best I can, if you would just listen to me!" It feels wonderful to yell, to let it out. I know I won't get through to her this way, but I can't stop.

"Enough of this, I can't stand to see you do this to your child. Think of the baby! What kind of mother…" she shouts, but I interrupt her.

"What kind of mother, what, Mom?" We're both on our feet now, yelling across the table at each other. "You want to tell me how much I suck as a mother? GO AHEAD! I already know it!"

"Who is not listening now, eh?" she snaps back. "I never said…"

"You didn't have to. I know what you think. Always assuming I'm screwing up or giving up. I'm not! I've never given up on Owen, not for one second. You're the one who has forgotten about him. You're the one who won't even say his name!"

Her mouth drops open, a small noise like a choke coming from her throat. I know I've hurt her now. The lines around her eyes deepen as she squeezes them shut, both hands pressed to her chest.

"Eleanora," she says, her voice quiet now. "How could you think…" But I'm not listening.

"Just stop," I say, forgetting that I haven't even told her the worst part. My voice is thick, and without thinking, I've put one hand protectively over my belly. I knew it was a mistake to come here. To think that love could overcome failure.

My dad is just stepping out of his car in the driveway when I slam the front door shut behind me. He raises his eyebrows, surprised to see me, but clearly catching my red face and angry tears.

"Ellie?" he asks, coming toward me. But I just shake my head, walking by him and I drive off, fuming. I know I've overreacted. I know she doesn't know the whole story, but I'm convinced it would only make things worse. The pinprick of hope I had mustered up after therapy is gone, and now I know I've truly blown it this time.

CHAPTER 22

It's hard to think of my father as something or someone separate from my mother. They are a matched set, like a cup and saucer. You just don't see one piece without the other. Dad leaves most of the talking up to Mom, along with the decision making. He is content to follow along with whatever she wants. He's figured out, after forty-three years of marriage, that keeping Maria Lazzari happy in the first place is far easier than talking her down once she's upset.

So, naturally, I'm surprised when his car pulls up in my driveway a few hours after I've stormed out of their house. I can't remember him ever having been at my house without her. I don't know what she's told him, but there's not even the smallest chance she has sent him over here to talk to me. That would be too close to an admission of wrongdoing on her part and hell would freeze over long before that happened. This means he has come of his own accord, perhaps even against her explicit direction. I can hardly contain my shock.

I let him in, and he perches awkwardly on my couch after carefully moving aside the blanket I've been buried under all afternoon. I try to smooth my hair a bit, but I can't do much about the fact that I'm a thirty-three-year-old woman wearing pajamas at three o'clock in the afternoon on a Tuesday. He doesn't seem to notice or, at least, pretends not to. Dad is a get-dressed-when-you-wake-up kind of man, down to the shoes, belt, and watch, regardless of his plans for the day. I scoop up the pile of wet tissues from the coffee table, at least, and shove them into the kitchen trash.

When I return, he wordlessly motions for me to sit next to him. I do and he puts an arm around me, pulling me close until my head is resting on his shoulder. The gesture is unexpected. He must be angry or, at the very least, extremely disappointed, not only that I've screwed up my marriage, but also that I've argued with my mother again. Surely some kind of reprimand or admonition is coming. But all he does is hold me there, not saying anything. He reaches over and takes my hand in his, and that pretty much sends me over the edge. I can't stop the tears. Or the sobs that follow. Suddenly, I've fallen apart, yet again, but at least this time I'm not alone.

When I'm cried out and the sobs have turned to little sniffles, Dad hands me a handkerchief–yes, an actual handkerchief, probably one of the last few in existence–to wipe my face. He leans back a bit so that we are facing each other.

"You want to tell me about it?" he asks.

I don't want to disappoint him. I've done it so much. But I don't really have a choice. I tell him about Daniel and about the baby. He nods slowly, his thick brows drawn together in thought.

"So, this is why your mother is upset," he states.

"Yeah, she thinks I'm giving up," I say.

"Are you?" he asks. "Marriage is a serious thing. Especially with children." I look away from him. I can't hide it anymore.

"Dad... Daniel is not the father of the baby," I say, my words barely above a whisper. The shame is too horrible. My father knows that I've cheated on my husband. The fact that it only happened once, that I have no memory of it, that Daniel was doing far worse, doesn't matter. Nothing will change what it makes me or how my family will see me. I can feel him tense beside me, and it's like a physical blow to my body. I want to crumble away, disappear, do anything other than have to look my father in the eye.

The silence stretches out. When I finally turn back to him, there is a tear on his cheek. His skin is thick and weathered, brown in spots from years in the sun. The stubble of his beard is almost all gray, stretching down under his chin, where the skin has started to get soft and sag against his shirt collar. The tear stands out against all of it, proof that I've done it. I've hurt him, hurt them all, too much. The realization that I will actually be alone floats over me, and it's surprising how calm I feel. I've known this moment would arrive and I expected it to sting more. Instead, it feels like I'm finally letting go, allowing myself to fall into the blackness that I've created for myself.

He squeezes my hand, pulling me out of my daze.

"Oh, sweetheart," he says. "I'm so sorry. I didn't know how bad things had gotten in your marriage."

I search his face, not entirely sure I understand what he is saying.

"I... I... it's ok...I didn't mean for it to happen." I don't clarify whether I'm talking about the affair or the baby. I suppose I mean both. He nods, his eyes still damp.

"Mistakes happen," he says slowly. "It doesn't mean you are a bad person. God will forgive you."

A small part of me rolls my eyes inside, but I keep my face still. I know this is his way of saying that he forgives me.

"What about Mom?" I ask.

"That will be a little tougher," he admits, one corner of his mouth lifting. He has lived with my mother for over four decades and knows her better than anyone. "She told me what you said. Your words hurt her, my dear."

I look down at the handkerchief I've been folding and refolding in my lap. My father's initials are embroidered in the corner in tiny stitches. My mother has made dozens of ones just like this for him over the years. I spent a lot of energy being embarrassed by the old-fashioned quirks they had like this when I was younger. Their out-of-style clothes, their accents, their not-quite-normal way of doing things. At the time it made them seem out of touch when all I wanted was for us to be like everyone else. I never gave any thought to how hard it was on my parents, leaving everything and everyone they knew to come here, being different from everyone around them. Once again, the guilt swims over me in waves.

"Look at me, sweetheart," he says. I meet his eyes. "We have not forgotten our grandson. We pray for him every day. We miss him every day. It has broken our hearts to lose him."

"But you won't talk about him!" I say, my voice breaking. "You never say his name. You never mention him. You took his pictures down, Dad." Now it's his turn to look away.

"I am so sorry, my dear." He pauses to gather his strength. "I had to do it. Your mother would spend every day crying, staring at them. She prayed in front of them for hours and hours, asking God to watch over him, to help us find him. She couldn't sleep. She wouldn't eat. I was so worried for her, for her health. She was getting dizzy all the time and having headaches that wouldn't end. I talked to her doctor and she was worried for her as well."

My mouth hangs open. I had no idea. I was so wrapped up in my own head at the time. I thought I was fighting the battle alone.

"So, I took the pictures down," he admits. "She was making herself sick. She was so angry with me. She didn't talk to me for weeks. After a while, she forgave me. She knows I was trying to help. But we speak of him in our prayers every single day, sweetheart. Every day, we pray for him to come home, and for you to find some peace."

I can't stand this information. I can't process it. My heart, so bruised and broken and cold, feels the tiniest bit of warmth knowing that they are thinking of him. Hoping for him. And not blaming me for losing him. I throw my arms around my dad's big shoulders and bury my face in the soft folds of his shirt. He holds me for a long time.

"Dad, what am I going to do about Mom?" I ask, finally pulling my face away. He kisses me on the forehead. I wipe my nose again with the handkerchief, and it strikes me just how much love is in every one of those stitches.

"I'll work on her," he promises.

But we both know it won't be easy. And she's not the only one I'm worried about.

When Geneva, Nathan, and the girls come home a few weeks later, I immediately ask if I can stop by. I need to come clean about everything, as difficult as it is. My sister is glowing when she opens the door for me, her skin browned by the Italian sun, her face relaxed and happy. I follow her into the kitchen, feeling only a little jealous of her vacation tan and the gorgeous Italian leather sandals she is wearing.

"It was the most beautiful place I've ever seen, Ellie!" she says, showing me photo after photo on her phone as we perch on stools at the kitchen island. "The coast was incredible. The views, oh my God, you would die! And the food," she looks at Nathan, who is leaning against the counter on the other side of the kitchen, for corroboration. He too looks sun-kissed and casually rumpled in that post-trip exhausted kind of way. "Right, honey? Too incredible. I've never eaten so many carbs in my life! You just have to. The girls loved it. Pizza every day!" she laughs.

"Where are they?" I ask.

"Upstairs, fighting the jetlag," she beams. "I'll call them down."

She moves toward the stairs, but I stop her. I'm not sure I can tell all four of them at once. Or even how to explain my situation to a couple of teenagers. Geneva turns to me, concern creasing her face.

"Are you ok?" she asks, gesturing for Nathan to pour me a glass of water. "How are you feeling?"

"I'm ok," I say, trying to keep my breath steady. "But there are a few things I need to tell you." They both take a stool on the opposite side of the island and give me their full attention. I could cry just from the kindness of this undistracted dedication. I don't deserve it.

I tell them simply, without a lot of detail. It's easier to get it out that way. They listen, both keeping their faces still. When I'm done, they exchange a quick glance. Then Geneva comes around the island to give me a tight hug.

"Oh my God, Ellie. I'm so sorry," she says. "Wow, I mean, that's crazy. But you will be fine. You know we are here for you." She leans back to look at me and I manage a tiny smile. "What did Anton say?" she asks. "Are you guys… like, a thing?"

"No!" I answer quickly. For a second, an image of Anton and I together flashes through my mind, but I dismiss it immediately. "I haven't told him yet. I'm still trying to figure things out on my end." It sounds like a flimsy excuse, but I just haven't found the courage.

"He's a good guy though, right?" Geneva pushes. "I mean, you've been friends for a while, so maybe…?"

"I don't know," I tell her. "We'll see, I guess. I don't really know how to tell him. I don't want him to feel, you know, pressured or anything."

"Maybe he'll be happy about it," Genny says hopefully.

I shrug, wanting to be done with the topic. Nathan comes over to give me a kiss on the cheek.

"Daniel is an ass," he says. My eyebrows shoot up. "Sorry, but I never liked the guy. Total snob. I think you are better off without him. Serves him right."

This is so unexpected that I actually laugh. Then I can't stop. Geneva cracks up. Then we are all laughing. I haven't really laughed in such a long time that I feel rusty, like I've forgotten how. It's a strange feeling. But a good one.

The girls appear in the kitchen wanting to know what is so funny.

"Long story," I tell them. Then I insist they sit down and tell me all about their trip.

They give me about as much detail as you can ever wring out of a twelve- and thirteen-year-old. But I don't care. I just enjoy watching them talk, tucking their shiny hair behind their ears, curling their long legs up underneath them, fiddling with their nails or with the small gold necklaces they both wear.

"Daddy got them for us in Rome," Mikayla tells me and comes over to me so I can see the four small gold stars on a narrow chain. Geneva and Nathan beam, so proud of the girls, still on a high from their time together.

For a second, I feel like I'm intruding on their space and I make an excuse to head home. Genny walks me to the door, asking about the baby.

"I'm ok. I feel fine," I say, very aware that my stomach is pushing out against the waist of my pants. I have been ignoring the discomfort of my clothes, all of which I am rapidly outgrowing. I had donated all the maternity clothes I wore during my first pregnancy years earlier after Daniel and I were married, leaving me with very few items of clothing that currently fit.

"Why don't we go shopping some night this week?" she says, eyeing my expanding middle. I give her a half smile and am about to slip out the door when the girls come running up behind their mother.

"Wait!" Audrey says, shyly handing me a small bag.

"For the baby," Mikayla adds, leaning her dark head against Geneva's shoulder.

I reach in and pull out a tiny white onesie with an Italian flag on the front. It's so goofy and touristy, but I love it and am so touched they have thought of me. I grab all three of them in a fierce hug and turn to leave but stick my head back in a moment later, a thought occurring to me.

"By the way." They turn to me, their long hair swinging in unison. "It's a girl," I say and shut the door behind me. I can hear their happy shrieks as I walk to my car, and I can't keep from smiling.

CHAPTER 23

The girls are so giddy over the little socks and baby dresses and tiny pajamas that the Target baby section has on display they don't notice the sweat that has gathered at my temples or the way my hands are shaking so hard that I have to keep them shoved in my pockets.

"We're going to need a cart," Geneva says, sending the girls back to the front of the store while she steers me towards the racks of maternity clothes. She looks elegant as always in fitted black pants, a loose sky-blue button-down top that makes her look both casual and important at the same time, and short wedge boots that only highlight her long dancer's legs. I, on the other hand, am pretty psyched that I washed my hair today and have managed to cram myself in a pair of formerly loose jeans, which are currently being held together under my t-shirt with an elastic hair band looped around the button. I stand rooted in one unhappy spot while she starts to flip through the racks.

"Ok, what do you need?" she asks. "Shorts? A few loose shirts? Maybe one of those tank tops that helps support the weight of your stomach? I've heard they are fantastic. They weren't a thing when I was pregnant!"

She holds a few things up, asking for my approval. But everything looks boxy and maternal, and I don't want any of it.

Genny reads the look on my face and puts her arm around my shoulder for a quick squeeze.

"Come on," she says. "You might as well be comfortable." I let her gather a few items but refuse to try them on.

"I'm sure they'll be fine," I mumble as she sighs at me. We go to find the girls in the baby section, where they have already filled the cart with swaddling blankets, stuffed animals, and horribly impractical baby clothes.

"I'm not sure an infant needs a bathing suit or a glittery dress for that matter!" Genny says, taking control and sorting through what the girls have chosen. She adds some newborn diapers, wipes, burp cloths, diaper cream, bibs, and footed pajamas.

I wander away as she starts comparing Baby Bjorns with the fabric slings that let you tie your baby on to you in a variety of different configurations. I move through the crowded racks of clothes, fingering the soft fabrics, trying to remember bodies tiny enough to fit in them.

But the dresses and *Mommy's Little Girl* onesies don't catch my attention. Instead, I'm drawn to the pajamas that look like baseball uniforms and the dinosaur t-shirts and tiny blue sweaters. Owen was born in April, an unsettled time in New England. So his closet was full of an assortment of clothes to match the unpredictable weather. One of my coworkers even gave me a tiny yellow rain slicker as a gift—completely ridiculous for a baby, but so adorable that everyone ooh-ed and ahh-ed over it. Owen had outgrown it before I ever thought to put it on him. He often seemed to double in size overnight, having outgrown drawers full of clothes every time I went to dress him.

Now all of Owen's baby things are in boxes in my attic. I had saved them, not knowing at the time if I would have more children or not, and not having the heart to get rid of them after knowing I wouldn't. I picture myself climbing the steep attic stairs, pulling the boxes down and sorting through each and every memory of my son in his first weeks of life, sorting out which clothes would now work for his sister. It made my stomach hurt to think about it.

Half-sister, a voice in my head reminds me. But I push the thought away. Owen is mine, completely mine, and always would be. The same is true for this little one. But something inside me stiffens at the thought, holding me back from thinking of her as the same as Owen. Jane's words come back to me, urging me to allow myself to love this child, to let my heart open again. But I don't know how to do it. I feel shut down and angry, and I want to be anywhere but here, surrounded by baby things, forcing me to acknowledge my situation.

I pick up a tiny outfit that looks like something a rock star would wear. Little skinny stretch jeans, a t-shirt with a skull on it, a soft faux leather jacket. I could see a Baby Gap model wearing it, little hair spiked up with gel, a stuffed guitar in his hand. *A girl could wear this*, I think to myself. *Why not?* I check the price tag, and my eyes fly open wide. *Ah, that's why*, I think.

It hasn't even occurred to me how much all of this will cost. *How the hell can I care for this baby when I can't even pay my mortgage right now?* Daniel has said that he will help until the divorce paperwork is filed, which should only take a few more weeks. A wave of panic floods through me as the girls run up to ask whether I prefer a stuffed hippo in a ballet tutu or the pink penguin with hearts stamped on its wings. Their faces are so full of joy that I manage a watery smile as I put an arm around each of them and jokingly tell them they are both hideous.

Genny joins us, pushing the full cart, and catches the look on my face. She sends the girls off on a mission for pacifiers and shoots me a look.

"Ok, now what?" she asks, her patience wearing thin. My face flushes red. I can't blame her. This is supposed to be fun, and I'm bringing everyone down.

"Genny... I can't afford any of this. You know that I'm not working right now, and I have to figure some stuff out..." I trail off, not looking at her.

"Well, I wondered how you were getting by," she replies, all business. "So, what's the situation? Do you have any savings?" I shake my head.

"I've used most of it up since I lost my job. I didn't have that much to start with," I mumble. Geneva and Nathan have done very well for themselves and obviously don't want for anything. She'd never let herself get in this position.

"Ok. I understand things continue to be tough for you." She means it kindly, but I hear judgment in her words. "But you need to take care of yourself and this baby. These are things you are going to need. And since you refuse to let me throw you a shower, then this," she says, waving at the overflowing cart, "will be my baby gift to you."

I shake my head and tell her it's too much, but she won't hear it. She grabs my hands.

"Listen, like I've been telling you for years, you have to get used to the idea that people love and support you," she says.

But I can't answer her because my throat has choked up with tears. I can't stand her charity. I can't stand being a burden to her.

"Ellie, please stop," she goes on. "It's not the end of the world if you need a little help. Everyone does sometimes."

"Not you," I manage to choke out. "You handle everything. Everything in your life is perfect."

"Oh please! I have help with everything!" She throws up her hands but I wave her away. "Ellie, are you kidding me?" She starts to tick off on her fingers. "I have a house cleaner, a landscaper, a grocery delivery service, a personal trainer, tutors for the girls because I don't understand their math homework, a marriage counselor, and a whole team that supports me at work. There's almost nothing I do by myself! Trust me, I get that I'm very lucky that I can afford to hire help for all of those things, but I couldn't manage ninety percent of it if I didn't!" Her words strike me into silence for a long moment.

"Wait, did you say a marriage counselor?" I ask, frowning, suddenly wondering if I've missed something that's gone wrong between her and Nathan.

"Sure. Marriage is hard work, and we are all so busy that we hardly have time to think about our relationship. So every other week, we sit with our counselor, talk about anything that's been bothering either of us that we've been avoiding, work through our disagreements in a safe space, make sure each of us feels heard. It's been wonderful for us and, I think, has helped keep us strong."

"Why didn't you ever tell me?" I ask, wounded but also a bit glad that maybe Genny wasn't as entirely shiny and perfect as I thought. She shrugs, pushing her thick black hair back over her shoulder.

"Because it's not a big deal. It's just something we do that helps us. There's no shame in it."

I let that sink in, thinking about my struggles in therapy, constantly feeling as though I was a failure for even being there. The girls reappear, stopping our conversation, but Genny and I exchange a quick smile, feeling as though, maybe, we understand each other a tiny bit better.

I convince everyone to weed down the cart a bit, removing some of the things I can live without (like, apparently now you are supposed to wear big, chunky jewelry that your baby can chew on? What's wrong with a teething ring?). And I manage to remove most of the maternity clothes while Genny's back is turned. She can get stuff for the baby, but I can't stomach the idea of her buying clothes for me. *I can get by without them*, I tell myself, wondering just how I'll survive at all once the baby gets here.

CHAPTER 24

The day of the 5K is hot and sunny, and Farlow Park in the center of town is crowded, impressively, with hundreds of runners. I feel the judgmental eyes of every single one of them on me, as they always are at these things. My pregnancy is obvious enough that people, complete strangers, come up to congratulate me. I nod quickly at each of them and walk away as fast as I can manage, trying not to come in contact with any person who looks like they might want to have a conversation. The probability that they will ask probing questions is too high. About the baby. About Owen. About what it means that I will have another child when I don't have my first one. Instead, I make like a giant sweaty ping-pong ball, changing direction whenever I see someone coming, bouncing around, and avoiding any direct interaction.

The sun is relentless, and I curse myself for forgetting my sunglasses in the car. I have to squint, one hand shading my eyes, which is making it hard to evade people since I can hardly see them coming. I've still shunned maternity clothes, and none of my shorts fit, which has made for a very uncomfortable July and August. Since I rarely leave the house, I've been getting away with pajamas and cut-off sweats. Today I'm sweltering in a pair of leggings and an over-sized T-shirt, cursing myself for being so stubborn and stupid.

Banners with Owen's face, perfect and frozen in time, line the edges of the park. I avoid looking at them, knowing he doesn't look like that anymore. I haven't seen his face in two-and-a-half years. It's such a hard truth to accept.

The trees and lampposts are tied with blue and white ribbons, Owen's colors, as chosen by Genny. He was only four. His favorite color changed by the hour. One week he was obsessed with orange. He would insist on wearing his orange astronaut shirt every day, and orange dominated all of his paintings at daycare. The next week it would be green or red or black. Every one his "most favoritest!" until he changed his mind again. But now he is remembered only in blue. Genny even chose a picture of him in a blue t-shirt for the banners and signs. Blue to remember my baby boy, even though I remember him in rainbows.

The race has drawn a decent sized crowd. Vendors selling snacks and ribbons and t-shirts — all benefiting the foundation — add to the festive atmosphere. Runners of all ages, as well as spectators and families, babies in strollers, kids and dogs, and a reporter or two from the local newspaper stroll about. But there are no media vans, no TV stations wanting to pick up a long-tired story about a little boy who's never been found. There is no update to share, nothing to add to what has already been said about him. It's partly a relief, partly a disappointment. For one small moment, I am thankful to Geneva for keeping my son in everyone's thoughts with these events, as much as I dread them.

Mikayla and Audrey find me in the water tent, hiding from the crowds. They are both in running shorts and Nikes.

"Are you guys running?" I ask. I didn't know they were planning to participate.

"Of course we are," Mikayla says. "I'm running and Audrey is walking with her friends." Audrey grins at me, rocking back and forth on her heels, looking very much the younger sister.

"That's nice of you," I say. "I'm sure you have other things you'd rather be doing." The girls glance at each other.

"Aunt Ellie..." Mikayla says, hesitating. "We wanted to."

"Yeah," Audrey adds. "We did. We miss Owen too, Aunt Ellie. It's nice when we get to do stuff like this for him." Mikayla looks bashful but smiles and nods in agreement.

Their words stun me into silence. I blink back the tears stinging my eyes and grab the girls in a quick, sweaty hug before shooing them off towards the starting line. I find a piece of paper–a flier listing the foundation's upcoming events–to fan myself with. Even in the shade of the tent, it's over ninety degrees and horribly humid. Beads of sweat roll down my back under my shirt, and the baby shifts nauseatingly in my stomach. Pregnancy in the summer is no joke.

Genny hurries by in head-to-toe Lululemon gear, looking like an Instagram fitness model, directing people where to go, shouting greetings and flashing smiles. Her hair is in a ponytail under a baseball cap, but her makeup is still perfectly done and there's not a gleam of sweat on her. She catches sight of me out of the corner of her eye and rushes over.

"Where have you been?" she asks.

I feel a massive wave of déjà vu. I'm pretty sure she thinks I actively try to ruin these events for her.

"Everyone's been asking for you," she adds.

"Sorry," I say, not feeling sorry at all. "It's just too hot." She instantly switches to protective sister mode. She has someone bring me a chair and a cup of ice.

"No, I'm fine," I insist. The attention she is drawing makes me dizzy and even more sweaty.

"You just rest here in the shade, ok? We don't want anything happening to you," she says, the concern clear in her eyes.

"Genny, STOP! I'm fine" I hiss to her as people stop to watch the fuss she is making.

"Ok, ok. I'll come check on you soon. I thought you might want to come join me at the starting line to give a few opening remarks..." but I shoot her a look that confirms that this is not something I will be doing.

She backs away, hands up in defeat. I wipe away the sweat beading on my forehead and wish to God I could disappear. My belly feels stretched and tight, the baby rolling from side to side as if she can feel my discomfort.

I feel a desperate need to get away from the crowd and stand up to look for an escape route back to my car. The view of the water table swims in front of me, and splotches of light cloud my vision. A stranger in an "Owen's Honor 5K Volunteer" t-shirt grabs my elbow to steady me. Embarrassed, I thank her before pulling my arm away and righting myself. This honestly can't get any worse. The air is so thick, I can't seem to get enough into my lungs. I close my eyes and draw in a big breath, hoping that everything will stop spinning long enough for me to leave.

"Ellie?"

A familiar voice cuts right through me and plunges a stab of cold fear into my stomach. It can't be. Not here. I turn around to see Anton standing in the water tent behind me. He's talking, but I can't hear him over the rushing sound in my ears. I can feel a flush of heat rise through my body as Anton walks toward me. He's smiling and moving in slow motion. I want to turn and run but I'm frozen in place even as my mind races and hot flashes of heat continue to spread through me. My hands flutter in front of my stomach, ineffectually trying to hide my belly.

He walks closer and spreads his arms as if to give me a hug. Just before he reaches me, I see his eyes drift down and confusion spreads across his face. *Oh my God, he knows.* He is figuring it out. I want to run. I want the grass to open up beneath my feet so I can fall in. I want to do anything but be standing here, watching the realization spread over his sweet face. But I am here, and I do see it. I see it through a tunnel as my vision narrows down to a pinprick and finally goes black.

When a pregnant lady faints, all holy hell breaks loose. When she is the known mother of a lost child for whom a massive event is currently being held, the entire world slams to a complete and shocking halt. Luckily, I've fallen backward, and Anton has jumped forward to half-catch me on the way down, or so I assume because my head is in his lap when I blink my way back to consciousness after what I hope is only a moment or two of blackness. Honest-to-goodness panic ensues as people yell for help, call 911, rush to find Genny, and bring water and ice and towels and anything else they can think of. My horror is so profound that I close my eyes again and wish with everything I have to disappear.

"Open your eyes, Ellie," Anton says, the panic clear in his voice. "Please, open them for me, ok?"

"I'm fine," I whisper and try to sit up.

"Hang on, hang on. Give yourself a minute. Does anything hurt?" I shake my head.

Dear God, get me away from here.

"ELLIE!" Geneva screams as she bursts through the crowd. "Oh my God, don't move! Are you hurt? What happened! Are you overheated? *Someone give me some ice*! Did someone call an ambulance? Ellie, don't move! *Give her some space, for Christ's sake*!" The crowd falls into order at her command, and she kneels beside me in the grass, clutching my hand and pushing the sweaty hair back from my face.

I push her hands away and try to lift myself off of Anton's lap, but my head swims, and I close my eyes until it stops. Voices rush around me, a cold cloth is placed on my forehead, and someone fans me with cool air. I feel it all from far away. *I am not here. I am anywhere but here.*

The baby kicks, shocking me back to reality, and my eyes fly open, startling the ring of faces looking down at me.

"Ellie?" Geneva asks.

"I'm fine," I say again and rub a hand across my eyes, trying to focus and push myself up. "I just want to go home." But I have a feeling that won't be easy.

Instead, Anton and Genny each grab me under an arm and hoist me into a chair. My shirt clings to my sides and stomach, damp with sweat, and I avoid looking at Anton. He's standing next to me, gently holding a wet cloth to the back of my neck. I try to convince Genny to go, that she needs to run the event and race, the start of which is now overdue.

"I'm not leaving you," she insists.

"I'll stay with her," Anton offers.

"Thank you, sir, that's very nice of you, but—" Genny starts, but I interrupt her.

"It's ok, Genny. He's... this is... my friend... *Anton*." I say, begging her with my eyes not to react. Her eyes fly wide open, and she looks at me, at Anton, at my belly, and back at Anton.

"Oh!" she says. "Oh, I... um... I... uh..."

Anton's face flushes pink, and he mumbles something about it being nice to meet her. The awkwardness stretches into silence, and Genny turns back to fuss over me for another few minutes until a pair of paramedics show up and check me over. No one listens as I insist over and over that I am ok, that it was just the heat, that I already feel better, and that I absolutely, positively don't need to go to the hospital.

I convince the paramedics and everyone else that I don't need to ride in the ambulance, but they insist, with no room for argument, that a pregnant lady who has lost consciousness must get medical attention.

"I'll take her to the emergency room," Anton says. My heart drops, but I don't have many options. Genny is almost in a panic at this point because she is now twenty minutes late to start the race.

"It's ok," I tell her.

"Ok, but let me know exactly what's happening."

She takes a nervous glance at Anton before hugging me and running off into the crowd. I can hear her voice over the loudspeaker all the way across the parking lot, apologizing for the delay, as Anton helps me into the front seat of his CRV. He cranks the AC, which blasts much needed cool air over my sweaty face and neck. I'm still horrified by what happened, but it's taking a total backseat to my panic about seeing Anton.

Luckily, the hospital is only a short drive away. Anton asks about twelve times if I'm ok, if I'm feeling dizzy, if I need anything. He casts furtive glances at me, at my belly, and at my ringless left hand that rests on my thigh, but I avoid looking at him and focus on not breaking into hysterical sobs or panicked laughter about the situation I have gotten myself into.

Once in the emergency room, they let me skip the line and go straight back into a small room. *At least pregnancy has that perk*, I think. I try to tell Anton that he doesn't have to stay, but he sits in the chair next to the bed and firmly takes my hand as a triage nurse takes my temperature and pulse and hooks me up to a fetal monitor. A doctor comes in, runs a few more tests and the conclusion is heat exhaustion. They want me to stay on the fetal monitor for a while, though, to make sure the baby is ok. When everyone else has finally left the room, Anton and I are alone with the steady, undeniable blip of the baby's heartbeat reverberating through the air. I can't avoid him any longer.

"Ellie..." he says, and my eyes mist over. Without meaning to, I clasp my hands over my stomach. "The baby... is it...?"

I nod, looking down at my stomach, seeing how my hands have made a protective screen. Though she still seems like a vague concept, instead of a real baby, I'm not sure I can take Anton's rejection of her. Because surely, that is what he will do.

What else can he do? I've been awful to him, kept this immeasurable secret, pushed him away.

Anton blows out a long breath, his head in his hands. The baby's heartbeat blips louder and louder. Finally, he looks up at me. His face is strained, but I don't know if it's anger or shock.

"Jesus Christ, Ellie, why didn't you tell me?"

But I don't have an answer. The truth is that I am scared. Terrified. Sick. Guilty. The truth is that I am afraid of what he will want. Afraid he will reject us, and we'll be alone, and I'll be responsible for another child, even though I screwed it up before. Afraid that he will want us, and we'll suddenly be a family, as if the completely different family I had two years ago didn't matter.

"I'm so sorry," I whisper. "I know that doesn't fix anything."

"I assume Daniel knows?" I nod.

"He left me." The words catch in my throat. Anton pushes himself up out of the stiff plastic hospital chair and paces the small room.

"Jesus Christ," he says again, and I hate myself for doing this to him. "You should have told me sooner, Ellie."

"I'm so sorry, Anton," I say again. The words feel very small. "I didn't mean for any of this to happen."

He sits in the chair again, pulling it closer to the side of the hospital bed. He grabs my hand tightly between both of his and looks me in the eye.

"You're sure, Ellie? You are absolutely positive it's mine?"

His face is close to mine, and I can smell him. The scent jolts a hint of a memory in me, and I feel warm all over. His sweet brown eyes search mine, and I nod. He takes a slow shaky breath.

"I know it's a lot to process," I say, grasping his hand. There is a tiny, miniscule flicker of hope in me that maybe I won't be in this entirely alone. *Anton is a good guy*, I tell myself. *He won't reject us. He will do the right thing, even if I don't know if that's what*

I want. Out loud, I continue, "But I don't want you to think I'm pressuring you or asking you for anything. I don't even know what's going to happen. I can't afford my house anymore; I don't know where we are going to live. I haven't figured anything out yet. But, well, it's your baby too, so I guess you have a say and can be as involved as you want..." I trail off at the pained look on his face.

"Ellie," he says carefully as if he knows how painful the words will be, and I brace myself. I know before he says it that the flicker of hope, just like every flicker I've felt about anything in my sad life, is destined to quickly burn out.

"Ellie... I'm engaged."

And, darkness.

CHAPTER 25

My mother is trying to save me, one meal at a time. Not a moment passes when the house, her house, where I now live, is not filled with the scent of cooking food. She and I are still on rocky terms, keeping mostly to ourselves, other than her non-stop insistence that I *eat a little something, yes*? She is determined to rebuild our relationship based solely on calorie count, because we have made little headway anywhere else.

I'm back in my childhood bedroom, which isn't helping anything. The movie posters and stuffed animals and Baby-Sitters Club books I filled my room with years ago are all long-gone. The Bath & Body Works Cucumber Melon scent that permeated everything I owned faded years ago. But the purple flowered comforter I picked out when I was twelve still covers the twin bed and the same matching curtains still hang in the window, making me feel less and less like an adult, let alone a grown woman about to become a mother for the second time, and more and more like a child. A helpless invalid, a burden. A waste of space.

I have been spending most of my time curled up on my bed, wondering what the hell to do. But I always come to the same conclusion: it's too hard. There are no good options. Sleeping is easier. I pretend none of it is happening, ignoring the massive belly that I have to curl around with a pillow between my knees to try to relieve the pressure in my back.

My house went up for sale last week. Owen's house. My things and Owen's things are packed in boxes in my parents' garage and stacked around me in my old room. And ever since I signed the papers at the realtor's office, agreeing to let them list the house, I have been kept awake by endless nightmares where Owen finds his way home and I'm not there. He knocks on the door in his mismatched pajamas, looking exactly like he did that night when I put him to bed, tousled hair and all, and a stranger answers the door, and he runs off into the night, panicked and confused, thinking his mother has abandoned him. It absolutely crushes me, but I don't have a choice. I'm out of money. I have no other options. I feel as though I'm cutting the last ties to my baby boy, giving up on him and on the life we knew.

The baby things that Geneva and the girls bought for me are still in the bags I brought them home in. I don't know where to put them. Daniel came and took some things from the house, some furniture and kitchen things for his new apartment. I don't know where it is. I didn't ask him anything about it. Just told him to take what he wanted, while I signed the papers he handed me from his lawyer. I didn't read them, but he told me they allotted him part of the proceeds from the sale of the house, because he had been paying the mortgage since I lost my job and helping to pay it for several years before that. I didn't argue. There is nothing to argue about. He did agree to keep me on his health insurance until I can get my own. But he wouldn't look me in the eye when he said it. I don't know if it will cover the baby.

I haven't been back to see Jane. I got an email from her when I missed an appointment, asking if I planned on returning. I didn't answer her. She called and left a message after that, saying she was concerned. I call her office after it's closed for the day and leave a message, saying that I needed a break. From what,

I'm not sure, but I know I don't have the energy to sit across from her and explore any of what is going on.

Anton comes over to see me several times. He calls. And texts. Asks about the baby. He tells me the story of meeting his fiancé, Nicole, and all about their whirlwind romance. They met at Starbucks. They both reached for the soy milk. He smiled; she smiled back. Like a fucking fairy tale. I would be sad about it, except that I don't have room to feel sad about losing Anton. Because I never had him. I'm not even sure I ever wanted to have him in the first place. It's just another steady reminder that I'm alone. And meant to be alone. Which is why I can't picture this baby arriving. Why I can't believe that I will get to have a lifetime with her, because that's not how things go for me. I can't imagine holding her or caring for her or loving her. But my heart twists every time I have that thought, because, of course, I already love her so much that I feel myself pushing her away since love always ends in pain.

I think Anton has probably been talking to Genny. They have the same concerned pinch to their faces when they look at me in my pajama-ed, greasy-haired glory. He says he doesn't know what to do, but that he's here for me, whatever that means. I don't know what Nicole thinks of the situation, but I can't imagine that it was good news to hear about your recently betrothed. In a not-so-proud moment, it made me giggle a little to think about him having to explain it to her. I feel maybe a bit of jealousy, when I work up the energy anyway.

Anton and I don't get anywhere in our conversations, because neither of us knows what to do. It doesn't help that my mother is usually only one room away, loudly banging pots and spoons, reminding me of her disapproval. She scowls at Anton as if he has deflowered me or ruined my reputation or something. Though she still saves plenty of blame for me. After several uncomfortable visits, Anton convinces me to go out for coffee. I reluctantly agree, only in part because, strangely, pregnancy has cured me of my aversion to coffee.

We sit staring down into our lattes–decaf for me–still not sure what to say to each other. The coffee shop is empty enough that we have some privacy for once, the cashier and the barista flirting with each other behind the counter, oblivious to the awkward couple at the table by the window. Anton sighs, but I don't look up. I hate myself for putting him in this situation. All of a sudden, he lets out a small chuckle. I look up, perplexed.

"I forgot to tell you!" he says.

"What...?" I ask. I can't imagine anything being funny at the moment.

"Did you hear about Barry?" It takes me a minute to realize he is talking about the former CEO at our old company.

"What about him?" I ask, taking a sip of my now-cold latte.

"Got caught for insider trading, apparently," he says, smiling broadly.

"No way," I say, thinking about Barry's expensive clothes and the Tesla he had recently purchased before leaving the company.

"Yup, probably gonna do some jail time."

"Wow, that sucks," I answer, thinking of Barry's two college-age sons.

"I mean, he was a nice enough guy and all, but I can't help thinking of him having to trade his Vineyard Vines button-downs for a prison jumpsuit. *Oh, this fabric is AWFUL,*" he mimics, and I can't help a small smile. Barry was always one to notice quality.

"Remember when Rose spilled coffee on his shoes in the office kitchen, and he almost fired her right on the spot?" he asks.

I giggle, thinking of how horrified the soft-spoken receptionist was when she knocked that cup over.

"Oh my God, yes! He freaked out about those shoes! Remember, it was like ten o'clock in the morning, but he was so upset that he left for the day?" I add, remembering the whole office bursting out in laughter as soon as the door closed behind him, and how everyone rallied around a tearful Rose, convincing her it was an accident and that she wasn't about to lose her job over it. I smile at the memory, thinking of my old colleagues. I hadn't been close with many of them, but, for just a second, I feel a twinge of nostalgia for the camaraderie of those people.

Anton notices my smile and tilts his head as if he's trying to decide something.

"What about Ruby?" he asks suddenly.

"What?" I ask, confused. "Who is Ruby?" He reaches across the small table and places his hand over mine.

"For the baby." He watches me closely for my reaction.

My throat feels cottony. I swallow a few times.

"Oh…" I say, looking down at my lap, which I mostly can't see since my stomach has exploded outward over the last few weeks. We need a name for her, of course. But until now it hasn't occurred to me that I would have to run it by anyone else. I hadn't known how much Anton would want to do with her, and now here he is, suggesting names. It is a lot to process. I take a deep, shaky breath. When I look up, he is still watching me, hope obvious in his eyes.

"I hate it," I say, and he bursts out laughing. He grabs the edge of the table, doubling over. I grab at the lattes, afraid that they will end up on the floor, but he only laughs harder. I stare at him as if he's lost his mind.

"Ok," he says, wiping his eyes. "What have you got then?"

"Oh, I don't know…" I trail off. I mean, yes, I've thought about it, but whenever I say a name in my head, it doesn't feel like it could be the name of the actual human growing inside of me. "I guess I kind of like Nadia. Or maybe Camille?" Anton wrinkles his nose.

"They sound like old ladies."

"Older than Ruby?" I say in mock horror.

"What?" he says. "It's retro!"

He smiles that big smile at me again, and I actually feel a piece of my heart melt, just a little. We trade more ideas back and forth, not landing on anything solid, when his phone buzzes on the table between us. Without meaning to, I look down at the lit screen to see a text message from Nicole, who is saved in his phone with a little red heart emoji next to her name. He drops my hand, and I quickly fold it with the other one under the table, as if to deny that it had been misbehaving.

Anton clears his throat as he slips his phone into his pocket and tries to restart the conversation, but the moment has passed. I make an excuse for needing to get home, and we both stand.

"Ellie, I don't want to push you on anything, but we have some decisions to make besides her name," Anton says. "Like, can I be there when she is born? When will I get to spend time with her? How will we handle everything?"

His voice trails off, but I can see that he's excited. He is happy about the baby. I feel a little flutter near my heart. He wants her.

"I know," I say. "I just... I don't know. I'm staying with my parents. I don't have a job. I'm not sure about anything." I watch his face fall a bit. I know he's frustrated, but I don't have a plan. Or any real idea about what I want. He nods, though, and I follow him out the door.

He walks me to my car and opens the door for me. Before he closes it, he crouches down beside me and cautiously puts a gentle hand on my stomach. I'm surprised by this sudden closeness, and my belly clenches in reaction. Anton's eyes light up.

"Was that a kick?" he asks, excitedly.

"I don't think so."

"Oh." He looks crestfallen. I take his hand and press it to the top of my stomach where the skin is smooth and firm.

"That's her head," I tell him, repeating what the doctor told me on my last visit. I pull his hand to the other side and down a bit. "This is usually where she kicks." We wait for a moment, barely breathing, and I silently ask her to kick for her daddy. My stomach clenches again at the thought. *Your daddy…*

"She must be sleeping," he says, pulling his hand away.

I can hear his phone vibrating in his pocket again, and he flashes me a small smile before saying goodbye and closing the door. He trots off to his car, and my eyes fill with tears. I'm not even sure why this time, other than I hate that it's so hard. I wonder if things would be different if he hadn't met someone. Would we be trying to make us into a family? Would he want me as much as he wants the baby? Would we all live together in Anton's apartment?

I try to picture a changing table next to his leather couch, which is a weird thought considering I don't even have a changing table for her. I don't have a crib. Or a car seat. Or anything other than what Genny has bought me, plus Owen's baby things, which I still haven't worked up the courage to go through. Packing up his room was heartbreaking enough. Each Lego brick and stuffed animal was carefully organized and packed away, though Genny did convince me to donate most of his clothes. I kept some things. His Spiderman sweatshirt. The little shirt and tie he had worn to my parents' house on Christmas Eve. And, of course, the pieces of the pajama sets that match the ones he was wearing the night he went missing.

I had held his pillow up to my face before I took the sheets off the bed, desperately trying to smell the little boy scent of him. But it had long since faded away. In fact, his room felt cold and unused. Owen's spirit, which used to fill the room with light and excitement and life, had been taken away with him. The bright colors looked dim and worn and sun-bleached, even though his shades were always drawn.

A panic rose in me, as he slipped another step further away. I was forgetting the feel of his skinny arms around my neck, his body warm and soft against mine when I held him. *What a sorry excuse for a mother,* I told myself. And once again I was torn between the struggle of thinking of him all the time—filling my waking hours with memories and hopes and the soul-crushing truth that I don't know where he is—and the truth that he is less and less real to me. I know that the more time passes, the more likely it is that I wouldn't even recognize him now that he is older and probably so changed from the little boy I knew.

"Don't touch it!" I shriek at my mother, the edge of Owen's sheets clutched in her hands. Her shocked face stares back at me.

"I'm just changing the bed," she says, not understanding. "So he has clean sheets when he comes home." I practically push her out of the way, grabbing the blankets from her and smoothing them back over the small twin bed. I pull the pillowcase tight so that the superheroes settle back into place.

"No," I tell her, trying to calm the hysteria I hear in my voice that has only gotten worse and worse in the week that he's been gone. "Just leave them, please," I say, arranging his stuffed animals in a happy line across his pillow, all a blur through the tears in my eyes. I feel her small, strong hands on my shoulders, trying to calm me, trying to keep me still. But I can't stop moving. I can't stop trying to set things right, keep things the way they were a week ago when Owen was here, safe in this bed.

"Sweetheart," my mother says, trying to pull me to her. I know how badly she wants to help. How badly everyone wants to help, but we are running out of things to do. We've searched and searched, put out AMBER Alerts, begged for his return on the news, made posters of his little face, given his description over and over and over. We'll keep

searching. Teams are still out there. Police are doing traffic stops and looking for little brown-haired boys.

But all of it is out of my control, and I feel my grasp on sanity slipping, just like my son has slipped away from me. I crumple to the floor of his room, a little toy soldier, half-hidden under the bed, digging painfully into my knee. My mother sits on his bed and draws my head into her lap, stroking my hair. But she says nothing as my tears soak into the fabric of her pants. Because there are no more platitudes, no more reassurances. All we can do now is wait. And hope that he, somehow, is found.

CHAPTER 26

I return home after coffee with Anton, feeling as lost as ever, with the added pressure of knowing that I have to give him some answers. I half-notice that Geneva's car is in the driveway, but I'm still lost in thought when I walk through the front door. Mom and Genny are sitting close together on the couch, a faded photo album stretched across their laps. Genny looks up sheepishly and tries to close it before I can see.

"What?" I ask her, annoyed at the way she is acting. "What's that?"

"It's nothing, honey," she says, putting on her happy face and trying to get up from the low, aged sofa.

"Bullshit," I say, causing my mother to gasp in horror, as if she's never heard the word before. I walk over and try to take the album from her, but my mother puts out a hand to stop me.

"Here." She pats the sofa next to her, and I reluctantly sit, having to lower myself awkwardly onto the sagging cushions.

Geneva settles back onto the other side, and my mother opens the album to reveal a scattering of half-faded photos that have seen better days. Mom is in them, in flowing maternity tops and a fabulous 70s feathered haircut, next to my dad who looks tall and strong, with a full beard. They look young and relaxed, despite my mother's obviously advanced pregnancy. She flips the page, and there is baby Geneva. Perfectly round and sweet, dressed in impractical, frilly baby girl dresses and bonnets.

"You were the sweetest little thing," Mom says fondly, touching the tiny baby face in one of the pictures. "Such an angel!"

She reaches over and touches my sister's now forty-year-old face, still beautiful and smooth as ever. This is typical. My mother has always spoken of Geneva as if she was the perfect child, flawless in every way. This opinion of her has never wavered. And it grates me now as it always has, and I fold my arms across my chest. I'm about to make some excuse to run away to my room when my mom continues.

"I thought I would die having you though," she says nodding, and Geneva looks at her, shocked.

"What do you mean?" she asks, and I have to bite my lip to keep from smiling.

"Two days I am in labor with you!" Mom says, throwing her hands in the air. "Two days! The doctor thought you would never come out! Your poor father. Wouldn't leave the hospital. He was so exhausted he could barely stand. And I thought I would die from the pains." Geneva looks hurt.

"You never told me that," she says, defensively. Mom shrugs.

"What is there to tell? This is a woman's job: to carry the burden of children. To birth them, to care for them. This is God's plan for us," she says, and I stiffen beside her.

I see Genny's eyes flick over to me to see my reaction. I know my mother isn't aiming her words at me, but I can't help but feel her judgment through them.

"There are plenty of other things that women carry," Genny says pointedly, a hand on my mother's arm, as if trying to warn her not to upset me. Mom shakes her head.

"Too much! Jobs and charities and these yoga classes and activities! You are too busy, *cara mia*. Think about your girls. They need you," she says to my sister.

I push myself up off the couch in one hasty, slightly awkward movement, knocking the photo album to the ground. I know she isn't talking to me. She isn't trying to hurt me. But it's all too much; all the things I hate about myself. I was too busy; I was too distracted; I didn't appreciate what I had when I had him. At least Geneva hasn't lost her children. The anger, unstoppable and illogical, flows up and out of me.

"Oh my God, would you shut up, for once? She's doing an amazing job, and she's incredibly successful! You should be so, so proud of her! Not judging her for going to yoga or raising money for my son's charity! How can that possibly be a bad thing?" I yell, not seeing the irony of standing up for Genny's charity that I barely tolerate myself. My mother narrows her eyes at me and purses her lips together but doesn't say anything. "I'm the one you are actually disappointed in, so let's not kid ourselves. *I'm* the horrible mother. *I'm* the one who's not 'carrying the burden,' like I should be, right? Or like I should have done for Owen."

"That's not what I…" Mom begins, but I cut her off.

"Let's just be honest. I'm the fuck-up," I scream, taking joy in seeing my mother flinch at the word. "I'm the failure. I failed you. I failed Owen, and I'm failing this baby too. They should take it away from me as soon as it's born so I don't lose this one too, right? That's what you are all thinking, isn't it?" I turn to rush down the hall to my room and see my father standing in the doorway of my parent's bedroom, drawn by all the yelling. The pain on his face almost breaks me, but I push past him, one hand on my stomach, and slam the door to my room, shutting them and their judgment out.

As expected, shortly thereafter there is a soft knock on the door. I expect it to be my father or Genny, trying to soothe the hurt my mother and I have caused each other. But instead, my mother walks in the door and sits gingerly on the edge of the bed.

"Did you know," she says softly in her accented voice, "that I almost didn't make it to the hospital when you were born?"

I haven't heard this before, but I keep my back turned, not ready to give in.

"By the time I left your sister with the neighbors and your father drove us to the hospital, you were almost ready to come out." She puts a warm hand on my arm. "I was so scared that you would be born in the front seat of the car." She lets out a small laugh. "It was a brand-new car! Your father would have been so mad!"

I smile, in spite of myself, thinking about my father freaking out about blood and afterbirth on the upholstery.

"But we made it," she continues. "And they put me in the bed, and a few minutes later, you were here. So easy, compared to your sister. Such a sweet little baby, you were." I turn to see her face, to see if she is being sincere.

"I mean it!" she insists. "You were a wonderful sleeper. You ate so well. Such a precious, easy baby. Not like your sister at all."

"Yeah right," I say, still reluctant to go along with her story. "You always talk about what a miracle she was, what an angel."

"Of course," she says. "Every child is an angel." She rests both hands on my stomach. "Every child," she repeats more softly.

It occurs to me for the first time that this new baby is the same mix of love and fear for her that it is for me. I recognize in her eyes that heart-wrenching combination of emotions that I feel all the time now, and I feel horrible for not seeing it before.

"But your sister never slept, didn't want to nurse, had the colic, always crying. I was so exhausted, I didn't know what to do!" She smiles down at me. "Sometimes, I think, the second child is so much easier because God is giving the mother a break. She has already been through such difficulty when she is a mother for the first time that He makes the second baby calmer and happier. You were both my angels. My miracles. I can still remember your tiny fingers and perfect little face. So much joy you brought me." My heart squeezes in my chest.

"And now, so much pain," I whisper. My mother draws my hand up to her lips and presses a kiss to my fingers.

"*Cara mia*. God gives us both. We must decide for ourselves what we will do with it."

"I'm sorry, Momma," I whisper, squeezing my eyes shut.

"So am I, sweetheart." She leans down to press her forehead against mine.

My mother leaves me to rest. I can still hear Geneva talking to my parents out in the living room, and I wish she would leave. The stress of the day has given me a stomachache, and I just want to sleep. I must drift off eventually, because when a knock sounds at the door a short time later, it jerks me awake. I'm certain that it's Genny coming to say goodbye. But I'm exhausted and stay curled around the pillow.

"I'll text you later," I call through the door. The baby is doing flip flops and won't settle down. She twists and turns, making my belly lurch and stretch painfully. Another knock on the door, and I'm about to tell her to go away when the door pushes open.

"Eleanora, come quickly, please," my mother says. I am surprised to hear the sharp tone in her voice and a flash of worry slips through me.

"What? Why? What is it?"

"Please, come," she says, one hand clasping the gold cross she wears around her neck. She looks back down the hall toward the living room. "The police detective is here."

I understand her words. I know what she has just said. Detective Luzcak is here. But it takes a long moment for the reality of it to reach my brain. And when it does, a cold shiver runs through my body, and my belly tightens painfully. My eyes meet my mother's, and she holds out a hand to me. I get up from the bed, and my vision spins with blackness. I have to take her arm, leaning against her small frame to keep myself steady as my mind races. She holds my gaze for a moment, our fight from only moments before forgotten. I walk down the hall, feeling like I'm moving in slow motion. The hallway seems endless. Again, my belly lurches and tightens, as if trying to hold me back. Trying to keep me from reaching the end of the hall.

Detective Luzcak is standing in the living room, surrounded by my parents' aging furniture and faded carpets. He is in plain clothes. A blue sport coat over jeans. He has recently gotten a haircut, which makes him look like a kid on school picture day. Behind him, my father stands with one arm around Genny. She looks, for once, not like her usual composed self, but like a scared little girl, and I have a sudden memory of us as children trying to scare each other by telling ghost stories with a flashlight in the dark, past our bedtimes. I was always better at scaring her than she was at scaring me. I meet each of their eyes as I scan the room, still moving slowly as if time has somehow become thicker and more viscous.

The look on the detective's face is grim, and as he starts talking, I notice the lines around his bright blue eyes, thick and tan, and I assume he spends too much time in the sun, drinking beers on his back deck or mowing his lawn. He is a handsome man, and I wonder for the first time what his story is. Does he have a wife? Children? He doesn't wear a wedding ring, but not all married men do. Divorced maybe. Maybe he works too much, and that isn't conducive to marriage. I don't know much about this man. In fact, right now, I can't even think of his first name. Jason maybe? Or Christopher? We are practically strangers, despite the time we have spent together over the last few years. There wasn't time in those meetings for small talk, for getting to know one another. He had a job to do. I did as well. Yet, somehow, this man has become very involved in my life, present at my darkest, most horrible moments.

Like this one. This moment, where even though I feel dizzy and separated from reality, where spots of light float before my eyes and my feet don't seem to be resting on the ground, I am memorizing every detail. Mom's and Genny's cold mugs of tea on the scratched surface of the coffee table. The grass stains on the knees of Dad's gardening pants. The pain in my hand as my mother's wedding rings dig into my skin as she squeezes harder and harder, as if trying to stop our hearts from breaking any further.

The lines around Detective Luzcak's eyes deepen with sadness as he speaks. Because even though this is just a job for him, it's a hell of a hard thing to do. He'll remember this day as well but will try not to think about it too much. He can't let the job ruin him. He did his best. He tried everything to find Owen. And, in the end, he did. He and his team of expert child-finders. They found him. But, Detective Luzcak explains in his blue sport coat standing on the beige wall-to-wall carpet in my parents' living room, his words like arrows eventually reaching me through layers of fog and hysteria, they did not, in fact, find him in time.

CHAPTER 27

I go away. I go away from the words and the truth and the cruel things they tell me. About who found him and where. That it's clear now that he was taken. That someone, some terrible person has done this to him. That someone found the body of a young boy, buried in the woods and it's my baby, *my Owen*. My nightmare. That he was still wearing his mismatched pajamas and that's how they knew with certainty that it was him. Because if he's still in his pajamas it means he's been–*oh God, oh dear God*– all this time and I didn't know. My baby died and I didn't know. And I can't breathe as my head spins around all the words but more of them keep coming, from Genny and my mother and father this time, about how he can be at peace now. How we can lay him to rest. How he's finally been brought home. Too many words, and I don't need them, don't want them. So I go away in my mind to a safer, darker place, even while I lay crumpled on the floor of the living room in the house where I grew up, and where the arms of my family surround me like a halo.

I go away even as my body responds, fighting the knowledge that the worst has happened, rebelling against the truth. I go away hours later as my labor starts, six weeks early, and my water breaks on my mother's brown sofa where they have lifted me that night after the detective has left, and my father calls an ambulance because everyone is too distraught to drive.

I go away from the pains and the spreading open of my body as the paramedics wheel me on a gurney into the hospital. Though somewhere, from far away, I can hear my own voice screaming for my lost child as, clutching my stomach, I push away the hands of the nurses as they try to help me. But I don't want their help. They will take him away from me. I cry for Owen, begging them to bring him back, save him. I hear Genny's voice in my ear as she tries to help them lift me into the hospital bed. *'It's not Owen, Ellie. It's your daughter. Your little girl, she's coming. Ellie-belly, please listen, I'm right here with you. It's time to have your baby girl.'*

But she's wrong. I have a little boy. She knows that. My baby. My Owen. I can hear him; I can smell his hair. I can feel his body warm in my lap, safe in my arms. But then suddenly, I can see him struggling and scared. Terrified of whoever is hurting him. Calling out for his mother. For me. And I'm not there for him, even though I try so hard to find him. It's dark and cold, and I search for him, through fields and forests and empty buildings with hallways that lead to nowhere. I search and search, crawling on my hands and knees, tearing out my fingernails as I claw at locked doors and barred windows and dirt-filled holes in the ground, like the one where he....*Oh sweet God, no.* I failed. I let him down. He died knowing I wasn't there for him. Thinking I don't love him enough to save him.

I can't live with this truth. So I keep myself away from the surface, where these things are real, even as I fight and scream and the pains rip through me, and they pull my daughter, tiny and pink, into this horrible, horrible world.

Genny tells me later that I refused to hold her, even for a moment, before they brought her to the NICU. I wouldn't even look at her little body. I have no memory of this. She is premature and weighs only four pounds. Her life is at risk, but the doctors aren't clear about how bad it might be. Geneva's face is stiff as she tells me these things days after they have happened. But we are all wrecked with pain these days, so the time makes no difference.

They put my daughter in a plastic bubble with tubes and wires and a tiny pink hat with a bow on her head to keep her warm. They help her breathe. They help her eat. I don't see any of this because I am still far away in my mind, while my body lies rigid in the hospital bed, unaware of the post-birth pains and my milk-swollen breasts. I don't really believe she is mine. They swapped in someone else's baby to try to make me feel better about losing my son. Maybe the whole thing is a lie.

Anton comes and someone tells him about Owen, because he cries by my hospital bed and holds my hand even though I don't hold his back. He takes off his glasses and wipes his eyes. I wonder where his fiancé is. Anton asks me about the baby, but I don't know how to answer any of his questions. *He must hate me*, I think. I've done it again. Hurt everyone. Ruined everything. I don't speak to him. I don't speak to any of them. I am not there.

They bring me food, but I can't eat if I'm dead. *No*, a voice inside of me says, *you are not dead. Your son is. You know, the one you were supposed to take care of?* And a wail comes out of me as the nurses rush in, and my mother jumps up from the chair in the corner where she has been twisting the handle of her purse and wiping her nose on a handkerchief for hours, not knowing what to do. I watch, as if from the other side of a window, as my body arches off the bed, and I cry for Owen and beg them to make it not true.

Inside, I am detached and hidden, not letting this hysterical woman on the bed bother me. She isn't me. I wouldn't lose my child. *But you did*, says the voice, and the woman on the bed screams louder until they mix something into her IV that makes both of us very tired and we go far away to the safe place.

CHAPTER 28

One Year Later

My alarm is going off, and I know without opening my eyes that the clock reads 6:30, like it does every morning. The blankets on the bed are a little too warm, but I've slept with the window open just a crack, and I can smell the fall air, cool and earthy, drifting over me. I stay still for a few minutes, slowly breathing in and out, concentrating on maintaining the feeling of calmness. As much as I would like to, I don't hit snooze. I don't roll over to slip back into mindless oblivion. Instead, after a few minutes of concentrated breathing, I sit up, pushing the thick covers back, and turn the alarm off.

Before I've had too much time to think about it, I get up and walk to the bathroom for a shower. I brush my teeth. I comb my hair. Today I manage a little makeup and some deodorant. Back in my room, I dress in real clothes. Jeans and a slightly stretched out sweater that hangs halfway down my thighs. But it still counts. No sweatpants, except for the weekends or the really bad days. No pajamas, other than for sleeping. I've committed to doing all of this. We've all agreed it's for the best.

I walk downstairs, stopping for a moment halfway down for a few more deep breaths. The kitchen is always noisy and a little overwhelming. Nathan is making coffee and packing the girls' lunches. Audrey and Mikayla are sitting at the kitchen island, eating their bowls of oatmeal. And Geneva is in the corner, perched on a stool next to the high chair, feeding my daughter small pieces of banana. She lifts the small rounded fork, making silly noises to get the baby to open her mouth, then uses the fork to boop her on the nose, making the baby laugh her amazing baby laugh. I walk over and smooth my daughter's hair, which is just now long enough to tuck behind her ear, feeling the warmth of her skin on my fingertips. I lean over and kiss her head and whisper, "Good morning," before Geneva gets up to hand me my pills and a glass of orange juice. I glance toward the front door, knowing my mother will be walking in at any moment. She comes over every morning just as Genny, Nathan and the girls head out so she can help me during the day.

My daughter's name is Evangeline. Evangeline Laura Lazzari. When it became clear that I was not of sound mind and wasn't showing any signs of returning to a comprehensive emotional state and my daughter lay tiny and nameless, attached to a million tubes and wires in the NICU, my family held some kind of emergency meeting in the waiting room of the hospital while I lay sedated and destroyed in my bed down the hall. Everyone cried, I'm told, as they bargained and brainstormed and rationalized naming a child without consulting her mother.

Once they had agreed to do it, however, everyone had an opinion to share. My father said her name should be Maria, after my mother, but no one else agreed, and he threw up his hands and sat quietly through the rest of the conversation. Nathan offered Riley or Lucy, but the girls rolled their eyes and said they were too trendy. Mom strongly insisted on Francesca, after her sister who had passed away in her twenties, but she was gently voted down. Finally, Geneva suggested Evangeline. The girls loved it and insisted they use it. Anton, who had been quiet up to that point, liked it and also agreed to let her be a Lazzari as long as her middle name could be his grandmother's. I guess everyone was fine with that.

Mikayla and Audrey call her Evie. They both kiss her goodbye and squeeze her tiny hands before they grab their backpacks and leave to catch the school bus, with Genny yelling reminders about their afternoon dance rehearsal and soccer practice. The girls are Evie's constant playmates and babysitters. My heart twists to watch them together. Their dark heads against Evie's auburn curls. Their lanky teenage awkwardness against her chubby baby legs and round belly. They are all so lucky to have each other.

I live in the guest room at Geneva's house. Evie still sleeps in her crib in Genny and Nathan's room. Everyone is very sensitive to how much sleep I get. The doctors stress how important this is. So Genny wakes with her in the night. Comforts her. Lays her back down to sleep and sings her lullabies. I would feel guilty about this, but I've been told it's for the best. And Genny has done so well with her girls, I can hardly complain. She has always been a bit better at everything than I have.

Geneva and Anton have shared legal custody of my daughter. I was deemed mentally unable to care for her, though the judge agreed to keep our case under special review considering the circumstances. A mother doesn't often lose one child the moment another one comes into the world. Looking back, I certainly don't blame anyone. Not the hospital staff, who refused to send Evie home with me after her stay in the NICU, nor the judge who reviewed the case, or even Anton, who just wanted to do what was right. He was very fair through the whole thing, considering that he could have easily fought for sole custody.

Every other Wednesday afternoon, Nicole and Anton arrive to take Evie to their place. She giggles and holds up her chubby arms to them when they get there, and one of them swings her up into a big hug. The other one shoulders the diaper bag, and they never forget to politely ask how I am doing. Fine, I tell them, regardless of whether I am or not. When they drop her back off on Sunday afternoons, they tell me about their adventures at the playground, the zoo, the aquarium, the baby gym. All the places I used to take Owen. My daughter takes her first steps at their apartment. They show me the video. I know I should feel jealousy. But instead, I feel grateful. Glad that they are capturing these moments and memories that I am often too low to focus on.

Every time they drive away with her, I feel equally devastated that she is gone — and have to quiet the part of me inside that screams at them not to take her — and relief that she is someone else's responsibility for a while. Then, of course, I feel guilty for feeling that way and scared that someone will realize my feelings and take her away for good. Jane has gently coaxed these admissions from me over time and tells me it's normal, that I have to work up to being comfortable with the responsibility of taking care of another child since I blame myself for Owen's death. But I am her mother, and I know I should rise to the occasion. I am trying. Every day is a little, microscopic bit better, but it is still hard.

Not that it is Evie's fault. She is perfect. Despite her sudden and early birth and subsequent stay in the NICU, my daughter is perfectly healthy. I thank God every single day for this as I put on her little outfits and give her baths. I touch her tiny fingers and toes. I watch her grow with utter amazement and gratitude. She says *mama* and *cup* and *Nenny*, which is what she calls Geneva. Each word or sound that comes out of her cherry blossom mouth seems like a miracle, and I'm convinced she's absolutely brilliant. Every moment with her is a reminder of Owen at that age, that same milestone — heartbreak and happiness all in the same instant.

The hardest thing has been reading stories to her. Sitting her in my lap, with her sweet head tucked under my chin, and reading her the same words I read to him. For months, my voice choked up and I couldn't get through them. A few books I put on the shelf in the back of my closet, because they were just too hard. No *Goodnight Moon* or *Pajama Time* for Evie. I just can't do it. But there are other, new books about fairies or Angelina Ballerina, the dancing mouse, that are just Evie's, and those are easier to get through. They are the hardest, most wonderful moments with her.

I love her with a depth that frightens me. Sometimes I look at her, the translucent pink skin on her cheeks, her long eyelashes, her tiny, cupped ears, and the love blooms inside of me, warm and shockingly strong. But then at times, it sinks like a bomb down into my stomach and turns to a fear so real and horrifying that I have to stop and hold on to whatever is around me, or else I'll fall. The medicine has helped to calm a bit of this fear, but it always lurks beneath the surface, telling me that every kiss, every story, every embrace might be my last moment with her.

Again, Jane tells me this fear is normal, considering what I've been through, that it might never go away completely. But she gives me exercises to try to make me feel better. Check the locks on the doors. Use the baby monitor. Repeat my calming statements. Follow my routines. Appreciate every moment with her. Remember that what happened to Owen was exceptionally rare. Remind myself that Evie is safe. Tell myself it wasn't my fault. *But, well, we all know better than that, don't we?*, the voices still sometimes whisper.

Sunday dinners are now at Geneva's house. It's easier than having to pack up the baby and all of her things. So my parents come to us instead, and they never arrive empty-handed. They are far too Italian for that. Mom brings trays of her lasagna or pots of meatballs or foil-wrapped loaves of garlic bread. There is always too much food and I'm always told that I'm not eating enough. My antidepressants mess with my appetite, so I'm hardly ever hungry. But I put the food on my plate and push it around and take a few bites to keep everyone happy.

We eat at Geneva's big dining room table with Evie strapped into her highchair and pulled up to the table. She is the center of attention, giggling and throwing food on Geneva's handwoven Italian silk rug. She can do no wrong in everyone's eyes. Even when she screeches or bangs her spoon on the table while my mother says grace and asks Jesus to watch after Owen's soul. Without fail, everyone's eyes flick over to me as she speaks, to see how I will take the swift knife to my heart that I feel any time I hear his name, adding to the million tiny cuts inside of me, too many to count.

I take them as well as I can, repeating the words Jane and the others have told me. *He's at peace. He's not in pain. We brought him home. He's with God.* And I try to believe them because I've promised to try. I've made a deal with everyone: if I make an effort. If I take my medicine. If I promise not to hurt myself. If I get enough sleep and enough to eat and get dressed every day and try to be normal, then I can be with Evie. Which is all I want. And besides, it makes me feel better that they aren't afraid to say his name anymore.

CHAPTER 29

On the Thursdays and Fridays that Evie is with Anton, and on Mondays when Geneva works from home, I go to work at my new job. I have been told that I have to get out of the house, that the world hasn't stopped spinning just because I don't particularly want to be a part of it anymore. I think this is vastly unfair but agree because it means that I am going along with the "fix Eleanora" plan.

Geneva is friends with a realtor in town. On my work days, I go into her office and help with contracts and other paperwork. It is all behind the scenes, so I don't have to speak to many people, only the folks at city hall on occasion when I need to pull property records and such. But they are usually too busy to try to make conversation, so I never get stuck talking about things other than business. This arrangement works well for me.

I get lost in the work—reading contracts, taking precise, orderly steps, following exact procedure. The laws of real estate are interesting to me, if not the most exciting. Rushni, my boss, mentions that one of the community colleges offers an evening paralegal program that her cousin recently graduated from. She says it only took him two years to complete, part-time, and that I should consider it because I seem to have a knack for contracts. I shock myself by looking it up online and I actually consider signing up. It's far from the sales side of things, which is a life I can't ever imagine going back to. I am not the same person who strode into medical conferences in four-inch heels trying to make a sale with a convincing pitch and a killer smile. Good God, who was that person? *Owen's mother*, a voice whispers in my head, but I shush it away. I'm different now.

But there are many hours that remain unfilled. With so many helpful hands at home, the laundry and grocery shopping are always being handled by someone else. The house is neat, the dishes are always done. I find myself with too much free time. Jane tells me this is no good, that having nothing to do will inevitably mean reverting to old ways—sleeping through the days, obsessing about the past, watching HGTV until I know every episode of *Fixer Upper* by heart. She encourages me to exercise, to go out with friends, to do some volunteer work. She is ecstatic when I mention the paralegal program. But all the rest sounds very exhausting to me. Not doing anything is far easier, and I have to constantly remind myself to try.

One quiet Saturday afternoon—with Evie at Anton's, Geneva and Nathan at Mikayla's soccer game, and Audrey out with a friend—it's not unusual that I find myself alone. The house feels big and empty when no one is home. Everything is white and clean, except for the loud pops of color that Geneva allows in concentrated, thoughtful places, like teal and navy throw pillows on the couch, the bright paintings of big red poppies on the walls of the dining room, and a basket of Evie's pink and yellow and green toys tucked neatly under an end table in the living room. The only thing out of place is my purse, which I've thrown on the kitchen counter. I sigh inwardly, knowing that it will annoy my sister if I leave it there, and pick it up to tuck in the coat closet. A piece of paper, folded in fourths, slips out as I grab the purse, and it lands on the floor by my feet.

I look down at it for a long time, knowing exactly what it is—a list of support organizations from Jane. For months, she has been asking me to reach out to these groups in order to find others like me and take refuge in the fact that there are people out there who understand what I've been through. I had taken the list from her, knowing full well that I wouldn't do anything with it. I can't think of a single reason I would want to. I pick up the paper and walk toward the trash, but the thought of Jane's carefully hidden disappointment stops me. I unfold the paper and scan down the list of websites. There's a lot of them. So many.

"Goddamn it," I say out loud to nobody as I take the paper with me up to my room, where I've left my laptop. At least I can tell her I tried and it didn't work out.

Everyone has encouraged me, from the day that Owen was taken, to find support, to look for people like me who understand what it's like to lose a child. I know to them it feels like a natural step in the healing process. But it has never appealed to me.

To humor Jane, I start with the first name on the list. And in only seconds, I am overwhelmed. They are all here. All the stories. So many children. So many devastated, horrified, ruined parents. I don't read any story until the end. Only skim them for words that dig like daggers into my stomach. Abducted. Taken. Abused. Murdered. Car crash. Accident. Shooting. Fall. Cancer. It goes on and on, but I can only take it for a few moments at a time before my eyes fill with tears and I have to look away to catch my breath. And I realize what an absolute fool I've been. Here are the people. Here are the ones who get it. They've been here all along. I haven't been alone.

A mom in Somerville whose ten-month-old son was smothered by her drunk boyfriend. A couple in Rhode Island whose eleven-year-old twin boys were killed when their school bus hit a phone pole and rolled over. A family of five in Connecticut whose six-year-old daughter died of neuroblastoma after being sick for over half of her life. On and on. And while my heart ached for the children, I mourned for the parents—

their lives demolished by the horror of losing their babies, just like me. Yet so many of their stories end with hope: the Connecticut family now raises money for kids' cancer research. The twins' parents have gone in front of the state senate to advocate for seat belts on school buses. The Somerville mom is carrying on for her other kids.

Their strength is overwhelming, despite their monumental losses. Suddenly, I want to know them, to understand them, to let them know they aren't alone. But doubt stops me. What do I have to offer them? I know I haven't been an ideal mother to Evie, that my heart is not healed enough, that I've only barely started to sort out my own life, let alone help or offer comfort to anyone else. I don't know what to do. A small button at the top of the screen catches my eye. *Keep In Touch*. I click it and enter my email before closing the laptop. I'm not entirely sure I want to keep in touch with anyone, but I also know that the small feeling of hope burning in my chest isn't something I want to let go of.

The next day, I get an email from a woman named Sarah Monahan, one of the support group's organizers. She said she recognized my name from my email address and wanted to invite me to an upcoming meeting that they were holding in the area. I quickly close the email and put my phone away, panic rising inside of me. Reading the stories online, safely at home in my room is one thing. Meeting the people they are about face-to-face is a totally different and completely terrifying thing altogether. Can I do it? I'm not sure. But what I do know is that I can't keep going on the way I am, surviving day to day by keeping my head down and feeling nothing.

I open the email again and, with shaking fingers, type back a short reply. I slowly let out a breath, close my eyes and hit Send. And one of the tiny broken pieces inside of me gently falls back into place.

Three months later, I sit at the front of a room. Hundreds of eyes burn into the back of my head to the point where I can't stop my hand from smoothing my hair over and over again. Genny grabs my hand to keep it still. Although I've volunteered for this moment, I'm shaking all over and questioning what the hell I was thinking. Nathan and the girls sit to the left of my sister. My parents sit on my right, with Evie happily snuggled up in my father's arms. I look down at the notes in my lap, trying to make the blurry, typed words come into focus. I know what they say, but I'm not entirely sure I'm ready to read them out loud. I'm not even entirely sure I believe all of them. They are words that flowed out of me, once I decided to write them down, but that flow was painful and soul-draining. They are the brightest parts of me, the most hopeful parts. And while I can't truly feel them in every moment, I am working toward them. And I know that saying them out loud is the best way to move in the right direction.

Geneva squeezes my hand, and I feel a flash of gratitude for her. Not only for being instrumental in making this day happen, but for everything she's done. Though it's taken me a very long time, I understand that starting In Owen's Honor was her way of processing the terrible loss of her nephew, a perspective I had known but hadn't been able to truly appreciate before. And the fact that her way of coping was to help other people only shows that she's a pretty amazing woman and sister.

When I came to her with the idea for this event, she was shocked into silence. She had tried dozens of times in the past to get me to speak about what happened, but I had always refused. If I spoke about it, it made it real. It meant that he was gone, and back then, I didn't believe it. But now the facts cannot be denied, as much as I have tried. When I was done explaining what I wanted to do and why, she burst into tears and hugged me for a long time before letting go and swearing to move heaven and earth to make it happen.

Turns out it took far less than that to pull together. The need for people like me to find each other, to be heard, tell our stories in our time, to not let the world forget who our children were was strong. And once I started reaching out to those families I read about online, others began to flood in. So what started as a simple part of my own step toward healing became a tidal wave. But now that the moment is here, I am anxious and proud and scared and horrified that the next step is to get in front of this crowd of people and tell them about the most terrible part of my life.

"What if they hate me?" I ask Jane a few days before the talk. "What if I tell them about Owen, and they realize that I'm a horrible mother and I have no right to stand in front of them?" Jane frowns at me. She has corrected me on this point a thousand times, but I can't help feeling it on occasion.

"So what if they do?" she says. "That's on them, not you." She can tell by my face that I don't find comfort in her words. She tries again. "Some of the mothers you have spoken to have lost their children to illness, right?" I nod.

"Cancer, mostly. One to the influenza. Another to a heart condition. Why?"

"What do you think of those mothers? Is it their fault?" I pull a face at her.

"Of course not," I say. "Those were unpreventable."

"A random act of violence took Owen from you. It could have happened to anyone, anywhere. We've talked about this quite a bit, but it really seems like a tough one for you." I smile sadly at her.

"If you are asking if I will ever stop blaming myself, I don't think so. How can I? I hear what you are saying. I understand the facts of what happened. But I know I could have prevented it. I *know* it. I made so many mistakes with him. I didn't pay enough attention. I was busy; I was selfish. I focused on Daniel too much. I was careless. I might as well have invited whoever took him right into my house." My voice shakes as I speak, and I can feel the rage and the sadness start to fall over me.

Jane reaches over and takes my hand. The big turquoise ring she is wearing is warm against my knuckles and her wrist full of wooden bangles cluck against my knee.

"Ellie, everyone makes mistakes. Maybe you did make some when it came to your son. Every parent does. Perfect parents don't exist. But it doesn't mean that you didn't love him. It doesn't mean that you were neglectful. It doesn't make you a bad mother. It makes you human. What's horrible is that, in your case, it really was just a random crime that ended up targeting your son. A sick person with a broken mind did this. Not you. We've been working together for, what, a year and a half now? In all of that time, Ellie, I have not doubted for one second that you love Owen. And Evangeline. And been a wonderful mother to both of them. Nothing has ever been clearer to me."

I take a deep breath and try to digest her words. They aren't new ideas. She has said them before, as has Geneva and my parents and Anne and even Anton. No one blames me. And as much as I know I will never stop blaming myself, it does help. A little bit.

CONCLUSION

Hello everyone. Thank you so much for coming today. My name is Eleanora Lazzari. I am thirty-four years old, and I live in Newton, Massachusetts. On February 9, 2015, my son Owen Robert Lazzari was kidnapped from our home. I put him to bed at 7:30 and went to take a shower. I came out of my room half an hour later to check on him, and he was gone. I had left the back door unlocked–a failure for which I will never forgive myself. The kidnapper took advantage of my carelessness and took my baby. The police were at my house less than an hour after he was taken. But whoever kidnapped him was gone. They walked into our home and stole him from his bed — a place that was supposed to be the safest in the world.

For weeks, we searched for him. We searched everywhere we could think of. His face was everywhere. On every TV station, on Facebook, on posters, in store windows, on telephone poles, everywhere. But no one had seen him; no one found him. And for two-and-a-half years, I went to bed every night not knowing where my son was. Not knowing if he was dead or alive. Not knowing if he was cold or scared or hungry. Not knowing who had him or where they had taken him.

It ate me up inside until I didn't know who I was anymore. I wasn't living. I wasn't even really surviving. I was moving through every day like a ghost, like a robot. Barely existing. Because who was I if I wasn't Owen's mother? I didn't know. Sometimes I still don't.

I lived only within my own pain. While I knew that my friends and family suffered from his loss, I couldn't see beyond my own hell to understand or acknowledge theirs. And so they dealt with it in their own ways while I wrapped mine around myself and hid from the world.

On October 7, 2017, Owen's body was found in the woods of New Hampshire. He was still wearing the pajamas he had on the night he was taken, which helped the police identify his body so quickly. As of today, the police do not have any leads. They do not have many clues or much forensic evidence to help them try to identify a suspect. So, all I know is that at 7:30 pm on February 9th, I gave my baby his last kiss and looked at his sweet face for the last time. After that is anyone's guess. But I have to live with the fact that someone took my child away from me–and I failed to keep him safe. If I had known it would be the last kiss I would ever give him, I never would have stopped. In my heart, I have never stopped. I still hold him just as close to me as I did in that moment.

That is my story. But it's not all of Owen's story. Because for four years before that, his life was filled with amazing things — superheroes and firetrucks, baseball gloves and stuffed animals, ice cream cones and bubble baths — all the wonderful things that are magic to a little boy. And no child-stealing monster will ever take those things away.

For a long time, I thought no one could understand what I have been through. I used it as a shield to keep other people away. When I opened up to this community of grieving parents I finally understood that I wasn't alone. So many of you have stories like mine... like ours. Or stories that are very different from ours but end in the same tragedy of losing your children. You'll never convince me that there is any worse kind of pain. And that pain is what brings us together now.

Because besides that pain, we also share many other feelings. Love, for our remaining children and nieces and nephews and godchildren. Hope, for a future when childhood cancer and other diseases are cured and neighborhoods and cars and playgrounds are safer. Gratitude, for the family and friends and strangers who have rallied around us in our absolute lowest moments. And, though it's taken me a very long time, I am finally starting to allow myself to feel those things that go beyond the grief and the pain.

None of it is easy. Every single day is still a struggle for me. Every single day, I feel the guilt and pain of losing Owen. But I also feel happiness. When I remember his little-boy laughter. When I think of how much he would love his baby sister. When my family shares their memories of him – something they couldn't do for a long time for fear of pushing me over the edge.

Standing up here is one of the hardest things I've done. Sharing my story is so terribly hard. Every time I tell it, I relive it over and over again. For a long time, I thought that was a punishment I deserved. On bad days, I still feel that way. But it took me a very long time to realize that there was also value in sharing it. That my loss could help others deal with their losses. I've spoken one-on-one to so many of the grieving parents and families in this room. And simply knowing that there are people in the world who understand what we are going through is a comfort. Nothing I can do will bring my son back. But I've finally found a way to share his life in a positive way. And I'm so very grateful to everyone in this room for allowing me to do that.

Losing my son has changed me. I don't know that I'll ever feel normal again, now I have stood over my child's grave. But I am ready. Not to move on. That is the most horrible thing you could ever say to a mother who has lost her child. There is no moving on, because it would mean leaving a piece of your soul behind, and that's not possible. But I'm ready to return to the living and make the most out of this life.

I am lucky to have had my son. He brought so much joy to this world. I will continue with the wonderful work my sister has done with our foundation, In Owen's Honor, to raise money for children's causes, as we are doing here today. I will take solace in connecting with this community of families, because I have found kindred spirits here. I will speak about my son with our family and not let his memory haunt us, but instead let it bring us happiness and peace. And I will teach my daughter all about her big brother who is up in Heaven looking down on her. And know that he is looking down on me too, loving his Mommy and wanting her to be the superhero he always thought I was.

Thank you.

ACKNOWLEDGEMENTS

This story couldn't have happened without the love and support of some amazing people to whom I'd like to show my unending gratitude. I owe every moment I've spent writing this book to them.

I want to thank my mother for being the very earth I have always stood on. There is no part of me that doesn't come from you. I owe my survival, my heart, my humor and every silly song that pops into my head to you.

I want to thank my father for being my guide and my mentor and for constantly putting books into my hands for as long as I can remember. I owe this book in large part to you, along with my knowledge of so many things, my belief that I could actually follow this dream to reality and, of course, my outstanding organizational skills.

I want to thank my grandmother, Muriel–one of the strongest people I've ever known. I hope you are dancing with the Rockettes in Heaven.

I want to thank my first-born child, for seeing the world in a completely different rainbow of colors, for amazing everyone with your waterfall of talent, for not ever accepting things that are unacceptable to you, and for making me a mother.

I want to thank my youngest child, for your enormously caring heart and artistic soul, for your uniqueness and creativity, for the determination to be exactly who you are, and for willingly accepting your role of always being my baby.

I want to thank my amazing stepson for becoming the third child in my life and making our family whole, for your musically witty charm, your dry humor and your cool unflappability no matter the circumstance.

Thank you to my brothers–my co-conspirators for so many years. How three such different people came from the same parents, I will never know, but I love you both dearly.

Thank you to my extended family for your love and generosity and to my friends and colleagues for your ongoing encouragement and kindness. Thank you especially to those who helped foster this passion and told me to keep writing–those words of encouragement often got me through. A huge thanks to the team at Black Rose Writing for helping bring this book out into the world and to everyone for coming along with me as this lifelong dream has finally come true.

And lastly, most of all, I want to thank my husband, my love, Jason. I'm so glad we both reached for the soy milk.

ABOUT THE AUTHOR

Jessica Maffetore is a New England based author whose short stories and poetry have appeared in several literary magazines. She has also been a guest columnist for the Fitchburg Sentinel & Enterprise. Jessica attended the University of Hartford for undergraduate studies in Public Relations and Journalism and holds a Master of Arts degree in English Literature from Fitchburg State University. When she is not writing, Jessica is training to run marathons with her husband, going for walks with her rescue dogs, being tolerated by her teenagers, working in her vegetable garden, and dreaming about where to travel next. Jessica lives north of Boston with her husband and three children.

NOTE FROM JESSICA MAFFETORE

Word-of-mouth is crucial for any author to succeed. If you enjoyed *Eleanora in Pieces*, please leave a review online—anywhere you are able. Even if it's just a sentence or two. It would make all the difference and would be very much appreciated.

Thanks!
Jessica Maffetore

We hope you enjoyed reading this title from:

www.blackrosewriting.com

Subscribe to our mailing list – *The Rosevine* – and receive **FREE** books, daily deals, and stay current with news about upcoming releases and our hottest authors.
Scan the QR code below to sign up.

Already a subscriber? Please accept a sincere thank you for being a fan of Black Rose Writing authors.

View other Black Rose Writing titles at www.blackrosewriting.com/books and use promo code **PRINT** to receive a **20% discount** when purchasing.

Printed in the USA
CPSIA information can be obtained
at www.ICGtesting.com
JSHW020031270624
65395JS00001B/7